THE GLOBETROTTER

ALFRED BALM

authorHOUSE®

AuthorHouse™
1663 Liberty Drive
Bloomington, IN 47403
www.authorhouse.com
Phone: 833-262-8899

Published by AuthorHouse 11/02/2021

ISBN: 978-1-6655-4118-3 (sc)
ISBN: 978-1-6655-4117-6 (hc)
ISBN: 978-1-6655-4119-0 (e)

Library of Congress Control Number: 2021921034

Print information available on the last page.

"To move, to breath, to fly to float, to gain all while you give
To roam the roads of lands remote: To travel is to live."
                                        Hans Christian Andersen.

"Why do we love the sea? It is because it has some potent power
to make us think things we like to think."
                                        Robert Henri.

For Phyllis, with love,
For Mike and Sherri
Roger and Tracy.

1

"Billy was a bit of a daredevil," said the man. "It cost him his life." He seemed to chew on those last words as if he pictured the tragic death of Billy still happening right in front of him.

Two men, well into the autumn of their lives, were sitting next to each other on a wooden bench in *Vondelpark*, centred in the heart of Amsterdam. The park is an oasis for its citizens wanting to escape the turmoil of the busy metropole. It was a balmy morning in spring. The tall horse chestnut, beech, and lime trees were butting out, and birds were busy searching for the ideal spot to build a nest, warbling loudly to let their presence be known. Rays of the morning sun penetrated sparingly through the trees, warming the bodies and souls of the two old men and throwing patches of light on the grass in front of them. Mothers with young children were already claiming a spot. The children were frolicking like newborn fillies, running after each other, tumbling or playing tag, their laughter somehow resembling the music of the twittering birds.

The man who just spoke, mentioning the tragic demise of Billy, wore a blue marine's jacket over a white turtleneck knitted sweater and a soiled skipper's cap. A small golden ring was pierced through his left ear. With his right hand, he brought a short-stubbed pipe to his mouth and sucked on it. It was empty; he spat on the ground. The back of his hand revealed the fading tattoo of an anchor. His weathered, tanned face wrinkled like a *Shar-pei* was adorned with a short white beard under his chin, but no moustache, like a whaler from way back when. It was a characteristic face that could serve well as a poster for Alaskan crab or curly-cut pipe tobacco. He carried the aroma of tar, hemp, and dried sea salt.

"Bart," he introduced himself to the man sitting next to him. They had never met before.

Beside him, wearing blue jeans and a worn-out winter coat fashionable shortly after the war, in awe of the old tar and his incredible narratives, sat Harry. He seemed to be as much a part of the park as the old bench that they were sitting on. Harry was a frail man now, but from his build, one could tell that he'd spent a lifetime labouring hard. His complexion betrayed the truth that these days, his ventures outside the house were rare. He listened breathlessly to the stories that Bart seemed to so easily be plucking from his memory, having so little to contribute to the conversation himself. He was sitting slightly stooped, with his upper body bent towards the storyteller so as not to miss a word.

Bart sat as straight as a hussar on his horse. Time did not seem to have had much of an effect on the old sailor. He still carried himself with confidence, straightened his shoulders, and held his head high. But the sea had carved its brutal ceaselessness into the many wrinkles of his tarnished face. His neighbour on the bench might once have been as tall as the sailor, but his back was rounded, and his head hung close to his knees while he sat as if he had erroneously closed his fly while his necktie was stuck between the zipper. It was the anatomy of an excessively worked human being.

"A nice boy though, that Billy. He signed on the same year I did on the *Merwede,* sailing for Batavia. He was not even sixteen at the time and a bit short for his age. Maybe that's why he always dare-devilled and pretended not to be afraid of anything, to overcompensate for being short. My mates and I teased him a lot but also sort of protected him. We were delivering a cargo of construction material and some general stuff to Gibraltar. The skipper found a berth right across from the *Wily Widow,* a harbour pub with a rough reputation." Bart knocked his pipe on the sole of his shoe as if to empty it. "Of course, we went there that night for a drink. The skipper warned us, *'no nonsense you hear, you get your ass in jail; you're on your own, I'm sailing.'* But you know how things go, there were a bunch of smart-ass Limeys from a British Clipper who thought they owned the pub because Gibraltar is English".

Harry thought, *how could I know? I have never been in Gibraltar, nor ever in any harbour pub.* "Then what happened?" he asked.

"Nothing at first, we were just staying at our side of the bar drinking beer, but you know British beer is different, no foam collar like Dutch beer and not chilled – a pint they call it. One of the British wanted to make fun of Billy, who did not drink beer, only a shot of rum. *'Too small to lift a pint, Tommy Thumb?'* he smiled at his comrades seeking acclaim for his joke. Willem, our boatswain who was with us and who always took Billy under his wings, put his glass down and straightened up smelling trouble. Billy looked straight at the joker and loudly said for everyone to hear, 'No, asshole, I just don't like to drink the queen's piss like you girls are doing.' The guy took a swing at little Billy, but the boats was quicker. He floored the coward with one mighty blow. Soon barstools were flying, and the Limeys found out to their peril not to mess with us.

Surprisingly, the scuffle didn't seem to bother the bartender, who'd kept cleaning the bar with a dirty dishcloth as if nothing happened. However, we soon found out why he'd acted so strange.

It was certainly not the first brawl in his pub. Sailors from all over the world on shore leave would get drunk, enter into an argument, and sparks would fly. At the first sign of trouble, he had called the police. However, the fight was soon over, and we silently claimed victory when a few noses on the other side were bleeding, and some eyes started to swell beautifully while turning purple. Billy hit the guy who'd called him Tommy Thumb smack on the muzzle after the boats had softened him up first, but when he triumphantly looked at me, another Limey tested Billy's skull with a pool cue, and he sank slowly to the floor with a dazed expression on his face. I just held the bastard by his throat; then the police arrived to clear the room.

The damage to the interior was reasonable; it wasn't exactly furnished in Tudor style. Still, we did not get away with it that easily. We were already happy that the police didn't take down names, but instead, all they wanted to know was the names of the ships we came from.

The next morning both ships were chained, and the shit hit the fan. Our captain was livid.

The bar owner presented his exaggerated bill to the police, and we had to fork up half, which took a big bite out of my pay, and there was no shore leave for us in the next port."

"Did Billy die?" Harry wanted to know, having listened intensively to the story.

"Billy? Hell no, why?" Bart reacted as if he was surprised by the question.

"Well, you said he was a daredevil, and it cost him his life."

"Oh yes, of course, but that was not then. A sailor goes through as many pub fights as a harbour whore through clients. No, Billy died of something more sinister, let me tell you."

A young mother behind a stroller passed in front of them, smiling a greeting at the two seniors enjoying a day out in the early spring. The sirens of a police car in the distance momentarily disturbed the park's tranquillity until it blaringly disappeared out of earshot.

Pigeons were pecking at the dirt in front of the bench, cooing in protest that no breadcrumbs were offered. Over in the grass, two rabbits were chasing each other, ignorant of people on the meadow, eager to do what rabbits do in spring. On a low branch of the chestnut tree across the path on the left, a squirrel was nibbling on something he held in little paws, barking protests at the passersby.

"What about you, Harry?" Bart wanted to know, "what did you do?"

"Me?" Harry uttered, taken by surprise, "Me, I didn't do much. When I was fifteen, I started working for the Parks Department. I like to be outside, and I sort of like nature. Every season is so different. Look at it now; even a month ago, you could sit here and think that everything, every tree or shrub, had died. Then it becomes spring, and it looks like God just created it all over again. Somewhere hidden deep in the trunk is life. It hibernates like a bear in its den. As soon as the sun warms the bark, it sucks moisture from deep underground, and the buds on the branches thicken. Then, reaching for the sun, they open up and unfurl brand new young leaves, like a butterfly from a pupa."

The old tar looked at his newfound friend almost suspiciously. *What the hell is he talking about?* he seemed to be thinking.

"You see these shrubs over there, those with the olive-green leaves? They are called Rhododendrons, we call them Rhododendron Ferrugineum. Those on the left are going to have purple flowers, the ones on the right are pink. I planted them thirty-two years ago when I was still with planting. Later I moved to maintenance, and when I retired, I was head of the department."

Harry paused to emphasize how successful his career had been.

"So you worked your whole life here, in this park?"

Harry chuckled, *a typical question for somebody knowing nothing about parks*, he thought.

"No, of course not. Once I was promoted from planting to maintenance, I also worked in the Amstel park in the South. It is different from here, though; there's more for kids to enjoy, like the park train, midget golf, a maze and a rosarium. The rosarium was my idea. I knew every shrub and every rose by name. It was a great deal of work, though, because kids would eat the ripe rosehips; they are sweet, you know, especially the Damascena, they actually make a preserve from it. But they often trampled the shrubs, and I would have to call somebody from planting to replace them."

He stared into the distance, remembering the great responsibilities he used to have.

"Once I was sent to the zoo to help them out, man, those were the days. I replanted a whole section at the aviary – you know, where they keep all the birds, parrots and peacocks and things." A melancholic expression appeared on his face when he recalled the pinnacle of his career.

Harry let his gaze wander over the plants around them as if he was still the chief of the maintenance department. He sighed.

"And the animals", he continued, "You only see these pigeons maybe and some birds or a squirrel or some rabbits, but at night the parks are for the animals."

"Animals?" Bart wondered, "What kind of animals would there be in a city park?"

"Oh, quite a few – foxes, for example, and deer. There's also ferrets and rabbits, as you have seen, and owls, woodpeckers, and sparrowhawks feeding on the field mice. Then, of course, those damned moles messing up the pastures, but we poisoned those."

Bart did not seem to be very impressed.

"Wanna know how Billy died?" he asked, but he didn't wait for an answer.

"It was in Gili Motang in the lesser Sunda Islands of Indonesia. But before I get into that, first I have to tell you about that trip." Harry nodded.

2

"Before I signed up with the *Merwede,* I had already done a lot of other things. I was born in 1936, and as a kid, I lived through the occupation of Holland by the Nazis. It was hard to find enough to eat and stay alive, but even after the war had ended, it was not easy either. The Canadian and American liberators were gone, and the country needed to be rebuilt, yet so much was destroyed that it took a long time before there was work for everybody. But then the craziest thing happened. The government, afraid that there would be too many people living in Holland, given how small it is, subsidized emigration to Canada, Australia, New Zealand and South Africa. Families with many children – and a dozen was not uncommon then – left the country by the thousands. But the resurrection of Holland went fast, and soon the country that paid to send its hardworking citizens abroad, to suffer perpetual homesickness, paid to import workers from countries like Turkey." He paused for a minute as if to gather his thoughts.

"There were other problems too. Before the war started, Holland was still a colonial power with significant economic interests in its overseas parts of the kingdom, Netherlands Indië, what is now Indonesia, the Caribbean and Suriname."

Bart suddenly looked at the face of the man he shared the park bench with.

"But hey, you must be as old as I am, so I am sure you remember." Harry just nodded so he wouldn't stop his new friend from talking.

"Anyhow, when the Japs had so easily occupied Indië, the locals found out that those mighty Belandas, as they called the Dutch colonists, were not invincible, and they wanted their independence.

But the queen and government thought different and wanted the status quo to remain, so they sent in the army. Mind you, this was shortly after the war, and Holland was still fulminating about its five years of occupation. Still, they sent in troops to suppress again the almost seventy million people of the archipelago. They called it 'police actions', but it was nothing other than a bloody war, justified on the basis of four hundred years of colonial domination and exploitation".

"My nephew died there, Bart", Harry interrupted, "he was shot by a plopper. My family thought he died a hero. In school, they told us those boys were dying for queen and fatherland, defending our *'Insulinde'* – the *Smaragd Archipelago* as our teacher called it – against terrorists and communists. The Dutch did a lot of good there, didn't they? I mean building roads, bridges, schools and hospitals. Didn't the Indonesian people love the Dutch living there?" Harry wondered.

"Sure, they loved them as much as we did those Krauts. No buddy, they were lying through their teeth to us, the government and those teachers. Your nephew never died for the country but for big business who did not want to lose the profits they made from slave labour. That's all it was, sorry, my friend."

Harry did not respond. He just kept his gaze on something in the distance, maybe thinking about his nineteen-year-old nephew, who never had a chance to grow up.

"Anyway," Bart interrupted Harry's contemplation. "Anyway, let me tell you about that trip. We were sailing for Batavia, or Jakarta as it is now called post-independence, with a load of mainly technical stuff, spare parts, electrical supplies and things. It was going to be my first trip through the Suez Canal, and I was curious as hell. You know about the Suez Canal, don't you?"

"Not much", Harry answered, which really meant, 'nothing'.

"Well, let me tell you. In the old days, to sail to Indië, our ships had to round the Cape of Good Hope on the southern tip of the South African Peninsula. To forage our ships, the Dutch established a settlement there, hundreds of years ago, maybe by Michiel de Ruyter or somebody. Anyway, some smart Frenchman, Lepsis or something, I believe, came up with the idea to dig a canal in Egypt to connect the Mediterranean with the Red Sea. A hell of a job, but in ten years with one and a half million workers, it was done. Mind you, almost one hundred and twenty thousand workers died from heat and thirst, cholera or typhoid and other diseases.

But shipping saved more than six thousand miles, and what used to take 20 days now only took 13 hours. Anyhow, we were going to take a load of copra back – it's a dried coconut that Unilever used to make margarine out of. So here we were, in Port Said. Man, I have never seen so many brothels! We had to stay on board, but whores were waving at us, making suggestive moves along the sidewalk of the canal. Surprisingly, going through it is less adventurous than we thought. You actually go through a number of lakes connected by a canal until you reach Port Tawfiq, which is near Suez. It turned out to be more the realization that you cut the trip to Indonesia so much shorter than during the hay days of colonialism that made it an experience. The Panama Canal, with its system of locks, is more exciting, but I'll talk about that later. The Suez Canal has no locks."

Bart pulled his worn sailor's cap a bit lower over his forehead as if he was staring at the horizon across the waves.

"But as much time as we saved not sailing around the Cape, it was still six thousand miles to Java, and at sixteen knots, it took us sixteen days. Man, what an experience to be in Indië for the first time. We were so indoctrinated about that tropical island paradise, and then to actually be there was something else! Walking under those palm trees, seeing those thousands of short brown natives in their slendang – a sort of printed cotton short skirt they call Batik and a kind of turban on their head. They were carrying goods unloaded from ships on their heads in rows like ants. Smelling the spicy air, hearing the sounds of the tropics, man, what a happening."

Bart sucked again on his empty pipe, seeing before his mind's eye again the busy harbour of Jakarta.

"We couldn't wait to test our sea-legs on solid ground. The first thing we did was buy some white cotton pants and shirts and a braided straw hat because, man, was it hot.

There were rows and rows of people in the harbour hawking all sorts of stuff like souvenirs, wood carvings, flowers, beautiful coloured stuffed butterflies, live birds, lizards and monkeys. People, especially women, were squatting on the roadside selling dried fish, fruit, fresh coconut, and many other fruits we didn't know. Some had a little sort of barbeque with a few pieces of smouldering charcoal in it, sitting on a flat stone on the ground in front of them. If somebody wanted to buy, they heated the fire with a bamboo fan, put thin bamboo sticks with pieces of meat on it, and then when it was cooked, they ladled over a peppered peanut sauce and served it on a bit of banana leaf. It smelled delicious and tasted good. We all tried it, but it was so hot that it burned our throat, so we quickly went for a 'Bir Bintang' that looked and tasted like Heineken. Then, of course, there was another reason we needed to cool our throat, but our heads even more. Quite a number of the local women were only wearing a sort of skirt, so we saw tits galore – and that after weeks on the ocean! To be honest, many were hanging on the woman's belly with dried nipples pointing at their toes. However, there were also the most beautiful women I've ever seen with boobs you still see in your dreams when you're back in Holland. Like the headlights on a Rolls pointing straight ahead."

Bart became poetic, a somewhat lascivious smile appeared on the old sailor's face, but he decided to spare his friend further details.

"Were you married? Harry asked.

"Married? Me? No man, no mooring line was going to tie me to shore. I am a sailor, not a landlubber. I was not born to have one woman. The sea was my land, the harbour pubs and brothels my home."

"I was", Harry commented.

"You was what?"

"I was married", Harry clarified. "To Anna. She was a fine wife and a good mother. She loved flowers and plants, and our daughter Hanny and our son Jaap when he was little. I met her when I was about eighteen while planting a field of violets, over there on the right," he pointed, "because it was spring. She was walking in the park and stopped to watch what I was doing. She told me she liked flowers, and I gave her a little bouquet of dark blue Viola Odorata. The next day she came back.

We married on my birthday, June 16th. We did not have much, but we loved each other, and for six months, we lived with her granny. I learned that both her parents had died in a bombardment during the war. God was that grandmother a bitch. I have seldom seen an old woman resembling a witch and acting like one as much as that creature did. If the inquisition had still been there, I would have volunteered to light the pyre."

In contrast with his eyes softening when he talked about his Anna, they changed to a look of intense revulsion.

"Whenever we were eating at the table in the kitchen, she would look from Anna's plate to mine and back while shoving the food in her toothless beak. But we bought the food and paid for it. Sometimes in the morning, when the bitch had maybe been putting her deaf ear against our wall the evening before, she would look at Anna like she beheld a giant turd. 'Viezerik', she hissed, meaning pervert. But we were married for chrissake! So I said to Anna one day, 'if we don't leave here, I'm going to kill that harpy'. Luckily Anna just found a job as a second maid with a family in West, so we found a small flat and moved in. Those were the happiest years of our life. We both worked, were frugal and could save some money.

Low and behold, when the old bitch died, Anna inherited two thousand guilders. Then little Jaap was born. We were over the moon. That nice family Anna worked for kept paying her even while she was home taking care of the baby. Later they became a sort of Godparents, they just loved Jaap, and Anna became first maid". He swallowed, "Then disaster happened.

The fire brigade never found out how the fire started, but among the ashes, they found the charred remains of Anna's employer and his wife. She was inconsolable, maybe because she had to grow up without parents and now losing that nice couple. For a long time, she was in a depression, but I could not help her, and God knows I tried. Then she became pregnant with Hanny, and slowly she recovered."

Bart listened with feigned interest. He didn't know much about domestic issues or family problems. With the pipe between his stained teeth, he looked at Harry, wondering why he had not just strangled that old bitch.

"Anyway, Anna found a new job as a housekeeper when the kids went to school and kindergarten, and I was promoted to maintenance with six men under me. We had a good life.

Jaap was smart; he was always in the top of the class. Hanny much less, but she was the sweetest girl a father could have and good looking too, taking after her mother. Although my Anna was growing – I ended up with twice as much as when we married – Hanny was slim as an elf."

Harry paused to take off his coat, it started to approach eleven, and it had warmed up quickly.

"Then suddenly my little Hanna was sixteen, it was as if I never saw it coming that she was no child anymore but a blossoming young woman. She went to discos on Saturday nights, and one day she came home with a boy. 'Dad, this is Ahmed,' was how she had introduced him to me." Harry made it sound like he just tasted something sour.

"I looked at the pimple-faced snotnose my princess had brought home. He was dressed in Salvation Army throwaways that seemed to be the fashion. His dark hair was longer than my Anna's. He resembled a weasel, or rather, a crossbreed between a weasel and a duck. I didn't trust him.

Hanna said he could play the guitar so beautifully. I wish he had kept his fingers on the strings instead of on my Hanna because four months later, Hanna was pregnant, and the weasel was gone. She cried her heart out, but what can you do? The baby was born, a little girl that, thank God, looked like her mother. We raised it together, little Corry, like she was our own. She comes to see me now, and Corry still calls me papa."

It was all Harry had to say. He just looked at his hands and was silent. They were large old hands. Thick blue veins were pushing against the transparent brown liver-spotted skin, and thick calcified nails never to be really clean again affirmed a lifetime of manually digging in rich Dutch soil.

3

"Java was interesting," Bart remembered. "Between the typical tropical dwellings in Jakarta are still plenty of buildings with Dutch sounding names, like *Apotik, Polis, Kantor Pos* or something on the façade, reminding of the old days. It would take six days before we'd have our cargo on board and need to return, so the captain gave us three days shore leave to see something of the country. There were large natural parks – you would have loved it – with volcanos and things and animals like tigers and rhinoceroses. Some wanted to go and see those, but I could go to the zoo for that. So instead, we went to a crazy old building completely made from grey carved stone as big as a pyramid. They call it Burubruder or Burabura or something. But there are a thousand islands, so why would we only stay on Java? Some guy said that Borneo was incredibly exciting and that there were still head-hunters there, wearing their dick in a long horn that they tied with a string from its point around their middle – you could still see their balls hanging. But I'd rather see boobs than balls, and of course, I needed my head for a few more years, so I said no. The guy was crazy anyhow because he was talking about New

Guinea, which is a completely different island. Now, Billy wanted an anchor tattoo on his arm, so we went to one of those guys first, not a shop, just a guy in the street with an old chair. But he did a good job, and Billy was as proud as a mermaid with a dick. From that point on, Billy considered himself one of the boys. He was still a virgin when he came on board, which you could never tell from the way he bragged. He had heard that girls looked at your feet because big feet meant a big dick, so he walked on shoes two sizes too big". The old sailor guffawed.

"There were hundreds of local guys calling themselves guides, trying to sell you trips. One had a picture of a real dragon, as big as a bus. 'What the fuck is that,' said Anton, our third officer who'd gone with us. The guide told us that they really existed, but only in Indonesia, in Gili Motang. 'Where the heck is that?' one of the guys asked. The guide showed us on a thumbed map. It was about a thousand miles east, close to the Sunda Islands, passed the island of Bali. That would take us way too long by boat, but dammit, to see *real-life dragons*, we thought. As it turned out, the guide had an idea. There were several daily flights with a Garuda Constellation to Flores. From there, going to Gili Motang by boat was easy.

Six of us decided to go, me and Billy, the third officer and three other guys. The rest wanted to go to Bali by boat. I didn't like that Constellation plane very much, but to be honest, it was a good flight and to see the archipelago from the sky was fantastic. The service on board from those small, slender, light brown stewardesses in colourful uniforms was perfect, and the food delicious but spicy – those stewardesses were too. You might not know it, but the Indonesian people smoke a funny kind of cigarettes with powdered cloves in the tobacco. It smells strong and sweet, but you get used to it, *krekketek* they call it. The plane was practically imbued with the scent of it. We landed at an airport called Maumere, which was way east on the island, but it gave us a chance to see something of Flores too; there's a lot to see there. We went to a crater called Kelimutu; I remember because I saved all the tickets. You won't believe it, but there were lakes in the mountains with water of different colours, red, blue, and green.

Of course, daredevil Billy wanted to dive in one of them because there was a sign strictly forbidding it. We also made a hike through the rainforest and over cliffs to reach a village called Wae Reboribo, I think. It is a traditional village with teepees built from reed. Only Manggarai are living there, very interesting. But our destination was Lenteng, way west of the island, where a boat was waiting to take us to Gili Motang and those pre-historic dragons. The boat was more a sort of large canoe, with a roof but open on all sides. Attachments were sticking out on port and starboard to stabilise the thing during rough seas. We were sitting on wooden benches; the diesel engine smoked and smelled like hell. I don't remember exactly how long the boat trip took us but sitting on those damned wooden benches, well, it was long enough. The water there is crystal clear, and we could see all sorts of fish. It was just the six of us in the boat that could hold two dozen, but it was booked for us in my name by that guide. Anyway, it was only forty bucks for all of us.

We soon approached what looked like a giant cone-shaped green mountain sticking out from the ocean. Gili Motang is only some twenty miles in all and uninhabited. We landed at a coral sand beach. The boat stayed out, so we had to wade knee-deep through the water with rolled-up trousers and shoes in our hands. To be honest, my heart was beating in my throat, and we looked over our shoulder at the boat, thinking, *stay close, buddy.*

Bart paused, rubbing the back of his hand across his mouth to remove spittle. He looked at the sky where a few clouds were assembling, threatening to cover the sun.

"Then what?" Harry asked, in his mind walking through the cool water to the beach.

"Nothing", Bart responded.

"What do you mean nothing? They don't exist, those monsters?" There was disappointment in Harry's voice.

"Oh yes, they do; you better believe it. But they're not exactly welcoming you at the beach to their island. Nor do you look for them with a bag of peanuts like you would for monkeys in a zoo.

The boat driver shouted at us, 'Tuan, perhatikan! Hewan-hewan itubarrabarra' or something, – that is Indonesian, it means *Sir, watch it! Those animals are very dangerous.*" He stared at his hands as if the warning in that strange language still reverberated in his memory.

"But we were there to see Kimono dragons", he continued,

"so we *were* going to see them. On the far side of the beach, the vegetation starts right away with dense shrubs and tall trees, and paths that are six feet wide are meandering through it to higher elevations. We decided to follow the path.

The light hardly penetrated through the foliage closing in high above our heads. Then, finally, we reached an open spot, but still no dragons, at least that's what we thought. There were only a few large grey rocks the size of a bus. Then suddenly, one of the rocks turned its ugly head in our direction. A huge forked tongue, like that of a serpent, flashed in and out of its closed jaws as if tasting our fear. Suddenly the monster opened his enormous maw and produced a blood-curdling hissing sound like the steam of a locomotive while staring at us with tiny hypnotic snake eyes. Its mammoth head resembled that of a dinosaur crocodile but much uglier. 'Holy shit', whispered someone in alarm. We wanted to run, should have too, but we stood our ground as if our feet had grown roots. Thick green phlegm was slowly seeping from its jaws. It was the scariest thing alive I had ever seen."

Harry did not move. He seemed to be frozen stiff, as if he himself was hypnotized by the monster. Both of his hands were firmly gripping the bench seat. Perplexed, he drank in every word of the man beside him who had stared death in the eyes.

"Then we noticed that the monsters didn't move; they were actually rather uninterested in us. After having stuck out his devilish forked tongue and hissed once, the dragon lowered his monstrous head again and didn't move anymore. 'Shit, that was scary', said somebody, 'my God, what a horrible beast, just like from pre-historic times. What would they eat? The island is tiny.' 'Maybe each other', the third officer said, 'or their own young, as I was told they do, in the village you come from.' Everybody laughed, and the panic was gone. We actually slowly dared to walk a bit closer to have a good look. Now we could see that there was one huge creature and two just a bit smaller but still gigantic. They look like a crossbreed between a lizard and a crocodile. 'I bet they can't crawl fast because they're just fat bastards', Billy said, who, as always, wanted to show off and walked in front of us, taking a few steps closer towards them. 'Watch it, Billy', I remember shouting, 'you never know, he may be faster than a hare with pepper up his ass'. But you know Billy, I mean, you know what I just told you about Billy – he was a stupid fucking daredevil. No matter how close he walked towards the Kimono dragons, they did not move an inch. They just kept a lazy gaze out of those serpent eyes on the short idiot approaching them."

Harry was mesmerized. It was as if the demons were lurking near him from behind the Rhododendrons he had planted.

"'Goddammit, Billy, stay back', shouted the third officer, but it was too late. The question of whether those heavy behemoths could run fast or not was answered in a split second. It was like the large one, the one that had thrown a hissing warning at us, exploded into action. We ran like we were in the Olympics but stopped when we heard a heart-wrenching scream behind us. Billy hardly had a chance to turn on his heels and run before that dragon was on him. He bit the poor boy in both legs, then, lifting his enormous head, held him up high like a dog would fetch a rabbit. 'GUYS, HELP!' cried Billy, but what could we do? There were still those other two Kimonos, and we had nothing to fight the dragon. I felt sorry for Billy, but I was mad at him for his tomfoolery. Who the hell did he think I was? Saint bloody George?"

Bart knocked the empty pipe on his shoe again as if hitting something much bigger and more dangerous than his left foot.

"But we could not let the monster eat our little buddy either, so we walked back as far as we dared and started throwing rocks. Now, I'm a sailor, not a quarterback, so I missed twice, then I hit him on the head. Not the monster, but poor Billy. Now the dragon tasted blood too.

Thank God one of our guys was a better pitcher than I was – he threw a rock that was a bulls-eye, or rather a dragon's eye, I should say.

It struck the eye of the dragon, and incredibly it dropped Billy and slid back to where those two others were still on the same spot. We did not dare to run but walked as fast and unobtrusively as possible to where Billy was laying, white as a sheet and bawling like a baby.

He was not badly wounded. The dragons have sharp teeth, but he'd just held Billy for a moment between his jaws before he dropped him. The most serious wound inflicted on him was the rock I threw; it had made a bleeding gash on his forehead. We carried him to the boat, 'Bart, I'm going to die', Billy cried. He had pissed his pants. 'You're not, asshole', I said, trying to console him. But I noticed the boat driver shaking his head with a worried expression on his brown face.

I later learned that it is the slime from the fangs that kills.

Billy became very sick very quickly. He ran a high fever, and the serrated cuttings on his legs started to swell and ooze a green liquid. We went back to Lenteng, but there was no hospital, so we had to go all the way to Maumere. Billy was now really sick, his fever worsened, and he vomited bile. The doctor needed just one look at him, he said it was a Komodo dragon bite, but I knew that already. They gave him some antidote, but the trip had taken too long. It was too late.

However, we also had another problem. The guys needed to go back to the boat, and without six men, the captain would be in trouble. So we decided that I should stay with Billy, and they would go back, reporting what had happened. We put all the money we had with us together, so I could pay the doctors and the hospital.

Two days later, Billy died.

I was devastated. I had liked the little bugger. Now, very dead in a hospital bed, he looked almost like a schoolboy. Why didn't he listen when we warned him?"

"What did you do then?" Harry asked timidly.

"I stayed with him until after the funeral. It was a very emotional event because there was almost nobody, only a few people from the hospital and me. I bought some flowers that I put on his grave. But that was it."

"Did you go back to the boat?" Harry wondered.

"No, I didn't; I decided to stay in Indonesia. I was sure the boat had left anyway. A ship can't wait for just one sailor that doesn't show up in time."

"So what did you do then? You got to live somewhere, find a job, I guess?"

"Well, that, my friend, is another story."

4

The clouds had drifted by, the sky had turned into a deep, bright blue, and the April sun was pleasant. More people sought to dwell among the spring flowers or just walk the park, inhaling the scent of spring. Bees buzzed above the flowers, sucking the first drops of nectar. A group of young girls in blue and white school uniforms walked by, giggling and chattering as they passed the old men on the bench, pretending not to notice the young boys following them and yet furtively making sure they knew. In the distance on the far side of the park, the bell of an ice cream car could be heard.

Harry took a watch from his vest pocket, attached to a button with a silver chain, but put it quickly back, never announcing what time it was. He did not want to miss a word of the stories the entertaining old seafarer sitting next to him told.

"You know nothing about Indonesia", Bart introduced his next narrative.

"Everything you were told in school was a lie. Mind you, those teachers had never been there themselves. All they knew and told us they just read in some book. But how can you then understand anything from a thousand island tropical archipelago? You can't.

How can you ask somebody to describe the taste of a banana if he only ate apples? You can't. As I told you before, there are maybe a thousand islands, big and small, and each of the bigger islands has its own population, its own culture and different languages. I remember in school, all we learned about 'Our Indië' was *Java, Sumatra, Borneo, Celebes, Bali, Lombok, Sumba, Sumbawa, Flores, Timor Klein Portugees*. The teacher would stand in front of the class with his pointer stick rhythmically tapping the islands depicted on the large map hanging in front of the blackboard.

In a monotone voice, the whole class would repeat, 'Java, Sumatra...' until we could dream it.

Then a story would follow about the fantastic accomplishments of our men and women in the colonies – the canals they were digging, the roads and bridges they built, the produce they grew like coffee, tea, pepper nutmeg, cinnamon, rice and all those exotic spices we sold to the rest of the world.

The teacher would then read a story about those primitive people that only spoke Malay. They'd detail how hard it was to educate them and how pleased they were to work for the Belanda's on the plantations or in the vast warehouses in port. They'd say how our dapper missionaries chased the devil out of their heathen hearts and brought them true Christian religion. They would also tell us about the horrible tropical diseases and how those poor people washed themselves in a Kali – a dirty river that was also used as a sewer. Many babies of those poor heathens died, and there were no schools for the young ones who survived, so they too worked on the plantations. Once the lesson about that tropical paradise concluded, we had to stand next to our wooden benches. Then, with the teacher swaying his hand as if swatting flies, we had to sing, *'Voor Koningin en Vaderland vecht ied're jongen mee'* (For queen and Fatherland every boy joins the fight). But of course, we didn't have a clue what we were supposed to fight for. Then a priest would come into class to remind us of the dire circumstances those poor children in the tropics were living under and cautioned us not to forget our weekly dime for the mission on Monday."

In his mind, Bart must have been standing next to his bench in school once more, singing again of how he would fight but wondering what the hell for. Then, finally, he stood up to stretch his stiffened legs, and a flock of pigeons fluttered up to land only a few yards further on the path, then trip-tripped back to where they started pecking at the dirt.

Bart sat down again.

"It was all bullshit, you know, we learned shit about what Indiè was really like and what those colonists really did over there. And we especially learned shit about how that beautiful faraway archipelago with twenty times the number of people Holland had, became *'part of our Kingdom.'* You know how?"

Harry shook his head, "No".

"Through bloody murder, my friend. The peaceful populations of those islands were violently oppressed. First by the Portuguese, then the British and lastly the Dutch, who had an ace up their sleeve called Van Heutz. He was a General, who, with violence and cunning, conquered Aceh and murdered many of its brave warriors, as well as their women and children. Paradise was now pacified, and the local population added to the long list of thankful devotees to the King or Queen of The Netherlands. Now nutmeg, pepper, cloves and cinnamon could be shipped to Holland and sold to the world at 400% profit. But because we owned most of those islands already, since the VOC in the seventieth century, and all those locals loved working 12 hour days for us at little pay and even less food, somebody smart thought we might as well grow cash crops there. Back in Holland, they had to pay fieldhands, but here they were cheap as shit. So soon, coffee, tea, cacao, tobacco, rubber, sugar and opium were grown on large plantations, all owned by Dutch companies, with white overseers. In large numbers, families from Holland decided to offer their services to the betterment of their country and, as a blessing to the locals, flocked to the islands. They lived like royalty with dozens of Indonesian servants too stupid to speak Dutch yet were great at serving while prostrated."

Harry looked at Bart with suspicion; he was undoubtedly exaggerating. The Dutch Indies had been a proud and important part of the Kingdom of the Netherlands. Those primitive populations there, those Malayans, were they not educated, converted to Christianity and introduced to Western civilization by the Dutch? The teacher in school had told him that they loved Holland; there must be something true about that.

"But there must have been nice people too there, Bart?" he hopefully suggested.

"Oh sure, and I met quite a few of them—especially those that were born there because their parents or grandparents immigrated. To them, Holland was a fata morgana, some abstract place their parents constantly whined about in the club, but it was the system that stank. The local population were treated as sub-humans with disdain at best and always exploited. There was a variety of great cultures; each island had its particular centuries-old traditions. Their artistic acumen was visible in their buildings, their carved utensils, their gamelan music and dance, the way they dressed, and in the way they built enormous, richly sculptured houses of worship to honour their Gods. For those who were willing to see, there was an inner civilization among most island populations and respect for their elders and ancestors. Putting side by side, most Dutch colonials looked like culture barbarians in comparison."

It was quiet for several minutes.

"She died", Harry suddenly sighed, answering a question nobody asked.

"Who died, whaddya mean?" Bart asked.

"I'll tell you."

5

"Anna couldn't take it anymore", a sad expression appeared on Harry's face. "She was not really sick, but lonely, disappointed, unhappy, and that did her in. You know Hanna was still a sweetheart, and little Cora was the apple of Anna's eyes, but they left. I was very busy; there was a big project in West and me and my men had to work there because it was going to become a new park for West and we knew about parks.

Hanna had found a job at The Bijenkorf, that expensive warehouse in the centre, as a sales assistant at the men's clothing department. She loved her job, and then Sjefke showed up.

First, he bought a shirt, then a tie, the next day he came back to buy socks, then handkerchiefs.

The other girls were teasing her, *'Hé, Manneken Pis has the hots for you'*, because Sjefke came from Belgium. Manneken Pis is that statue of a little boy on the market square in Brussels, with his willy in his hand, pissing in the fountain.

Anyway, he asked her to marry him, and because she already had Cora, she was happy to have a man, even that one, who was a bit ugly and the sexton of a church in Dendermonde,

Belgium." Harry stated the obvious, but it was clear that to him, Dendermonde was as far as Indiè.

"When she left, Anna cried for a week. She missed her daughter and especially little Cora. Me too, but I was working on a new park in West, but I told you that already".

"What about your son? You had a son too, didn't you?" Bart remembered. Harry hesitated as if it was too difficult for him to talk about his son.

"Jaap was a disappointing asshole", he fulminated.

"I told you already that he was smart in school, so he went first to college and then to university in Leiden. It cost us a lot of money, but when both Anna and I worked, we could save just enough to pay for his tuition. But Jaap became a member of the student's club – corps, I believe they call it, or dispute or something, and he was ashamed of us. Jaap had friends with rich parents, big homes on the coast and expensive cars. He never came home anymore because he found some girl whose father was a surgeon, and he was not going to let her meet his mother toiling as a maid to pay for his studies or his father, who worked on his knees in the dirt.

He became a lawyer, here in Amsterdam with an expensive house at the Keizersgracht, with three children, but we have never seen them.

Then one day, I was running late because we had received a load of Asteraceae, or Dahlias as you would call them, and they needed to be in the ground that day. When I finally got home, I found Anna."

There were tears in the old man's eyes, his lips quivered slightly, but his body did not move an inch. He sat like that for quite a while. Bart, who thought he could guess what was to follow next, just bit on his pipe and waited patiently for his neighbour to continue.

"She was not even in bed; she was on the floor next to it, and on the bedside table was a small box she used to keep sleeping pills in, but it was empty." He paused again, swallowing before he continued.

"Not a note, no goodbye, nothing. In the morning, I had a wife. Then, in the evening, a corpse. I panicked and didn't know what to do, so I called our doctor, who came immediately but only confirmed she was dead. I knew that already. The police also came to make sure she was not murdered, though they were gone in no time.

Jaap didn't even come to bury his mother, nice fucking lawyer and what a great example to his children. Hanna came with Cora and Manneken Pis, and the head of City Parks was there in a black suit. There were lots of flowers with ribbons, but what was I going to do with flowers and no wife? I had flowers enough."

Harry just sat there, feeling the hurt again and the deprivation. Bart allowed him a few minutes before he continued.

"I couldn't stay in Flores, of course. Not that it wasn't nice, but I would have to think of those goddamn monsters all the time and of dead little Billy. So I decided to go back to Jakarta and find out where I could get a job. That wasn't easy because most people were contracted in Holland and signed up for six years. Still, I wasn't going to work on a plantation or a factory anyhow, shit man, I'm a sailor, and that's all I know. But although everything there was dirt cheap, the money I still had was not going to last long. I got a refund for the unused part of my plane ticket, which helped because going back by boat cost much less, but it took a few days. Enough boats were going to Jakarta, though they all charged different prices. I found one that was owned or captained by a Chinese. It was an old piece of junk with hammocks instead of huts for its passengers.

I was on board on Monday morning, but it took till Wednesday noon for the boat to have enough passengers to leave. It was a colourful bunch of people. They carried sacks, boxes and baskets with all their belongings, dried fish, fruit and vegetables, and chickens, piglets, birds and roosters in a woven reed basket. Later I found out that they were for cockfights. I noticed several different costumes and languages, but most were speaking Indonesian – they call it Bahasa. There were two Chinese families with children and one Dutchman who told me his name was John Timmermans. He was a bookkeeper at a trading company in Jakarta. We took hammocks next to each other so we could talk. He was young, about the same age as I was then, and turned out to be a nice guy, a bit shy at first, but he opened up soon. He told me he had been in Indonesia for two years with the same company. He married a local girl named Sarina, who was the daughter of a Dutch father and an Indonesian mother. He showed me a picture, and she was a stunning beauty, small but very pretty."

Just how pretty was clearly visible from the expression on the old sailor's face.

"Anyway, the first day everything was fine, we found our corner and the other passengers allowed us some room. There was a small, dirty galley from where an old Javanese woman cooked a surprisingly tasty rice dish with chicken in a spicy coconut sauce, for which we paid very little. I was not used to sleeping in a hammock, so when in the middle of the night, the sea became a bit rough, and we were swaying from port to starboard, I was wide awake. I was maybe the first one who noticed from the sound that something was wrong with the old diesel engine. It was knocking like a cart on a cobblestone road. I knew, of course, what was going to happen – the bearings would fail, the overheated engine would be completely blocking the shaft. It would become impossible to pull the shaft and repair the engine on the ocean, and we would be dead in the water. That old Chinese captain was asleep, and a young motor driver who was ignorant of the trouble didn't speak a word of Dutch or English. I was finally able to let him know through sign language to wake up the captain, who started to fulminate in Chinese when he heard the engine, then boxed the poor boy's ears for not waking him up. It was soon clear that the man had no clue what to do next. Several passengers woke up and, realizing that something was wrong, started to offer free expert advice. But nobody knew a damn thing about diesel engines, so I decided to roll up my sleeves. John climbed out of his hammock too, and although he knew as much about engines as a nun knows about a catwalk, at least I could talk to him, and he knew enough Bahasa to translate. I soon found out what the trouble was, and lo and behold, in a case with rusted spare parts and rubbish, I found a perfect ball bearing. It took me half a day with the help of John to replace the damaged bearing, and when the captain restarted the engine, it was purring like a kitten. All passengers applauded, chattered, laughed and nodded approvingly while the Chinese captain pumped my hand. I could not pay for food anymore, people offered me fruit and drinks. When we arrived in Jakarta, the captain returned the passage money I paid."

"Could you find a job there?" Harry asked.

"Yes, but not immediately. John asked if I had a place to stay, but of course, I didn't, so he invited me to his home until I could find a job and a place of my own. Sarina was the sweetest girl ever, and she welcomed me as if I was an old family friend. However, I was not going to take advantage of their hospitality, so when I read an ad placed by a coffee plantation looking for a foreman in a local English newspaper, I went there. I was interviewed by an administrator, who had a concern with the fact that I had no experience, but when I explained that I was a troubleshooter, he decided to give me a chance. Then I found a small but comfortable house and a babu – that is a woman taking care of the house and you – and after thanking John and Sarina for their kind hospitality, I moved."

"Was it a good job? Did you like it?" Harry wanted to know.

"I did, but that is quite another story," Bart answered.

6

"Hanny came back", Harry mused aloud, "with Cora. Anna was already five years dead.

You would think a sexton should be a good husband and father, being in the church and things, but Manneken Pis was a sneak. He was drinking like a sponge, came home drunk, then started a fight with my princess, the asshole, while little Cora was crying for her mother.

He was almost fired when the priest discovered who drank the mass wine, but the priest gave him a second chance when the snake cried for forgiveness. Then the church found out that the shithead stole some of the money the parishioners offered every Sunday, and he was kicked out. But now, he drank even more and borrowed money from whoever was crazy enough to lend it to him. Finally, the fights became physical. If I had known that the coward put his hands on my daughter, I would have wrung his fucking neck."

Harry was still mad. He clamped his large hands together as if he could feel the scrawny chicken neck of Manneken Pis between them. He bit his under lip, then shook his head as if to wish away the dreadful thought of his princess being roughed up.

"But my Hanny is not stupid." He smiled. "One night, when he was in bed in a drunken stupor after having beaten her up again, she tied his hands together with one of his neckties, being very careful not to wake him up. She then took a poker and repeatedly hit his hands with all her furious might, breaking all his fingers. 'You drunken coward, try to hit me now!' she yelled to the bawling prick. Then she took all her belongings, picked up little Cora, who was with a friend that evening and came back home.

It was worse with Jaap," Harry carried on, "Jaap kicked himself off the pedestal he erected for himself. One of his student buddies, a bit of a loser but from a very wealthy family, started to deal in real estate. There's a lot of work for lawyers when those shady characters buy a whole city block where families rent apartments, then have them kicked out so they can sell the units at a hefty profit. City officials need to be bribed, crooked public notaries involved. Still, fortunes are made, so who the hell gives a damn that poor families are losing their homes?

Anyway, the smart-ass lawyer who was too chic for his mother and father doing honest manual work got himself involved in a big scam. Jaap lost his bar, I believe they call it, it means he could not be a lawyer anymore, and he had to pay half a million, which he did not have, so he had to sell his house and everything. His name was in the papers. That's when his wife took the kids and left him. I never contacted Jaap; I could not forgive him for how he treated his mother. Me, I don't care, but never wanting to see his mother who worked hard to give him an education, no, I couldn't forget that."

"What did you do, offer him a job in planting? Bart quipped.

Harry laughed, "No, he would not have lasted a week among my men; they were hard and honest workers but a bit of rough too. Now, tell me about that coffee job."

"You would never think when you drink your cup of coffee how much work is involved in the production. I didn't know a damn thing myself about it, of course, being a sailor, but I am not stupid and learn things very quick. Always had to because I didn't have much of a chance of an education because of my father, but I'll tell you about that later. Coffee only grows in a warm climate, and of course, Indonesia is hot like hell. The Dutch started the coffee culture there in late sixteen hundred, and I believe they imported seeds or plants from the Congo. You may think that those berries grow on a tree or like blueberries. But no, sir, you have to make rows and rows of holes in the soil and just before the rainy season, throw as many as 20 seeds in each hole. Why so many? Well, only half of them ever germinate. It takes several years before you have brushes that produce berries. Coffee grows as a berry; when it is ripe, it turns red, but then the trouble starts. Coffee has more enemies than friends, all sorts of pests, bugs, snails, birds and rodents. Not to mention the roots, stems and leaves are also attacked, but by other foes like caterpillars, butterflies and moths. Although the worst is a 2 mm beetle, they call it the coffee borer; it destroys half the crop worldwide.

There are only two sorts of coffee that are commercially important. One is Arabica, of which Indonesia produces 25% and Robusta, the other 75%. Robusta grows better in a hot climate like Indonesia. It is also more resistant against another problem, leaf rust, that can destroy an entire plantation. But Robusta is more bitter, and its caffeine content is 40 to 50% higher.

Now guess what the most expensive coffee is?"

Harry was not expecting a question, but not without logic he answered,

"Arabica?"

"No, man, you won't believe it, but it is shit coffee."

"Shit coffee? Are you kidding me, Bart?"

"No, my friend", the old salt laughed, "I am not. The most expensive coffee is called Kopi Luwak, and people don't pick it from the coffee plants by hand. They pick it from the ground under it. A small animal called a Civet, a bit like a cat or a rat, picks the sweetest ripe berries from the branches, eats them and shits the beans out. People collect the dried turds pick the berries out, and then after roasting, it becomes coffee that is twenty times the price of normal coffee."

"You're kidding me, are you not?" Harry's expression suggested that he would not be a taker.

"No, I am serious, but enough about coffee, let me tell you what happened there. The plantation was called Djampit, and it was old, built way back by the Dutch in early eighteen hundred. It was on high ground, about 1400 meters, which was nice because it was often a bit cooler than below in the evenings. I had to move from the house I just rented, but that was no problem, and I moved into a much nicer place with a porch and palm trees around it.

I did not have a clue what a foreman was supposed to do, but there was an elderly Scot who lived most of his life on the plantation who showed me around and explained things to me.

He told me that he dreamed of becoming a sailor as a young man, but he was stranded on Djampit, funny, eh? As it turned out, most of my duties were making sure people did their work. Alistair – that was the old Scot's name – called them lazy sons of bitches, but most of them were women.

I disagreed with that attitude. On board, there are always guys from far away countries, and you soon find out that we are all the same. Most of the other foremen, however, had the same attitude as Alistair. Still, they were the lazy SOB's and the people in the field were working their asses off.

Every foreman was responsible for a particular section, and my section was called Breda. I soon found out that there was a kind of competition for who's section would be the biggest producer. That was maybe smart from a manager's point of view, but some foremen were sadistic bastards and would beat the crap out of their workers to increase the berry picking, trench digging or other work. Now I gotta tell you one thing, I may not look like Mr Atlas today, but in those days, I was tall and strong as an ox, worked on board, built big muscles, and the pub fights taught us how to kick a guy's butt before he could say shit."

Harry had a close look at his new friend, and he believed him. There was something in Bart's attitude that told him as a young sailor he must have been quite a character and definitely not somebody to mess with.

"My workers, about a hundred women and fifty men, were observing me, wondering what kind of foreman that newly arrived Belanda would be. They soon found out.

I was there for about six weeks when, on my way to Breda, I passed Roosendaal, the section supervised by a German guy named Werner. It was noon and very hot; I remember my shirt sticking to my body. On the ground was a woman, old enough to be Werner's mother, and he was beating her mercilessly with a cane. The old woman was helplessly trying to protect her head with her thin bony arms. I was on the coward in a second, grabbed the cane from his hand and with my face close to his, I hissed, 'You do that once more, you goddamn schwein, and I'll break your kraut neck.' The workers just stared at us; as far as they were concerned, that never happened. Foremen would always cover each other's back. Of course, the people in the field did not hear what I'd told the weasel, but they got the message, and word went around among my workers.

That evening I was called to the house of the supervisor, who started to give me shit. I interrupted him. 'Sir, if my job here includes watching a young man beating an old woman senseless with a cane, count me out. Think of your own mother, sir, and imagine watching while a German sadist beats the crap out of her. Would you do nothing?' I think he silently agreed.

'That's not the point, Mr Bouman'', he said in a different voice, '"But if those pekerja sense disagreement between you foremen, then they'll take advantage of it – pekerja means workers in Indonesian.

'Sir,' I said, 'I will show you that my sector will outproduce all others, and I will never use force.' He looked at me without a word for a few minutes, then he said, 'You show me, Bart, you show me.' But I think that he thought I was bull-shitting him. Although the workers are not officially divided into groups, unofficially, they organize themselves, and each section has one man that they consider the *pemimpin*, the leader. In my sector, that was Kromo, a Sumatran, about forty years old, who had witnessed me dressing down Werner.

I told him about my meeting with the supervisor. He looked at me, nodded and said, *'Baik baik Tuan, itu akan terjadi'* – meaning *ok sir, it will happen."*

"And did it?" Harry wanted to know. In his mind, he had been walking among the coffee plants, watching all those beautiful brown women with their bare breasts picking coffee berries.

"You bet, at the end of the pluck, I was 40% higher than the next one, 40% mind you! But I smelled trouble. It was Alistair who warned me first. Watch your back, sailor, he said, you're making enemies. I forgot to tell you that every Saturday night, all of us foremen, the supervisor and some people from administration would meet in the cantina and drink beer, either Bintang or Jenever. Werner was sitting at a table with three colleagues whispering while throwing furtive glances in my direction. I got the message. I stood up at my full length, it was suddenly quiet in the cantina, and all eyes were directed at me. Some seemed to think, who the hell does he think he is, that rookie.

I took a big gulp from my beer, then said nothing for a minute to build up tension. 'I won', I said in a loud voice, directing my gaze at all of them. 'I won and not because I beat the crap out of my people like some here seem to enjoy doing. I increased production because I was in the field with my people, overseeing them and treating them like human beings. They noticed that and automatically were more at ease doing what they were hired for. Their baskets filled faster, as you all know by now. You may be trying to do even better than I did, but if the encouragement of your people means beating the shit out of them, I'll come for you, and believe me, you'll wish I never did.' I looked around the room at everybody, but I could see that they did not doubt my words. 'Now, if you feel that they slacken on purpose because they are guided by a softer hand, you come talk to me, and it will change. Enjoy your evening.'

I turned around, finished my beer and ordered another cold one.

The superintendent's eyes were on me the whole time as I spoke, but he did not say a word.

When, after the next pluck, it turned out that the production overall had increased 25% and there had been no violence, I was called to the administrator's office, the big boss of the plantation. When I entered his domain, he looked at me with a question in his eyes but invited me to sit down on a low chair in front of his elaborately carved desk.

'Bart', he said, 'I was told that you had something to do with the increase in production during the recent pluck. Your method seems to be somewhat unconventional in plantation terms. Still, your respect among workers and foremen is not the less for it. Therefore, I promote you to overseer. Keep it up, young man.'

Then he waved me away.

I was about a foot taller than the overweight bald administrator, who looked at the world through tired blood-shot eyes. His fat-cushioned small hands held a white handkerchief that he used to wipe the sweat from his brow constantly. He gave the impression that he had had enough of that godforsaken tropical hellhole. But anyway, I made quite a bit more money now, and I could ride one of the horses from the stables instead of walking around, and in our time off, we went shooting fowl and deer. I was a good shot, and my workers were happy with the meat I gave them. In return, they cooked me delicious meals, called Nasi-Goreng and Rendang. Too bad I was fired."

"Fired? Why the hell were you fired?" Harry was just getting used to the promotion and pictured himself high on a white horse wearing a white tropical helmet, riding along endless rows of coffee plants, surrounded by hundreds of half-naked pretty brown girls picking ripe berries.

"Let me tell you", Bart answered.

"That administrator might have been what he was, but his wife happened to be years younger. She was a real looker with long chestnut coloured hair, nice legs and even nicer tits that she didn't mind showing off. She had the hots for me, Jeanette did. I found that out when she kept sending for me to do all sorts of unnecessary jobs or asking my opinion about something. Then, while pretending to listen, she would bend towards me so I could not avoid staring at her gorgeous cleavage while trying, embarrassed, to hide my throbbing erection. But I wasn't stupid and was not going to lose my job screwing the administrator's wife, although she clearly wanted me to.

Then one night, I had just been to mandi – that's what bathing is called there – and was sitting in my pendek shorts in my reading chair with a book about pirates. The next thing I knew, my door opened, and there Jeanette was. She was wearing some kind of expensive yellow silk peignoir, and it was not difficult to notice there was nothing under it. *Jesus bloody Christ*, I thought, *trouble*. But my packer didn't agree.

'Want to help me finish this sailor boy?' she whispered in a sexy voice. She held a bottle of white wine by the neck in her right hand, leaning with her left against the doorpost. Her flimsy, sheer peignoir fell open. She smiled at my embarrassment. 'Are you going to invite me in, or do we fuck on the veranda?' she said.

She'd had a good start on the bottle already, I could see. Well, what more is there to tell, I'm not a saint, and she is a gorgeous piece of ass. She was a tiger in bed, holy moly, what a woman". Bart was licking his lips, staring with half-closed eyes at something in the distance.

Harry felt uncomfortable. He was not a stranger to rough talk, given the men he worked with, especially in summer with women in provocative dresses strolling in the park. Of course, he was not a prude either, but this kind of talk was not his cup of tea. *Well, I guess that's what sailors are like*, he thought and didn't comment. Besides, if he was honest with himself, he could picture himself on that white horse, so why not on Jeanette?

"Hours afterwards, while she was still in my arms staring satisfied at the ceiling, I told her 'we can't do this, Jeanette, your husband is going to fire my ass, and I may not be able to find a job in the entire archipelago when the story goes around. It was good girl, very good, but not again'.

She turned to me with an incredulous look on her face. 'Oh, come on, Bart, don't be so damned naïve. What do you think is happening here? Do you believe they are still dancing quadrilles here, holding hands bowing to each other? No, man, they are fucking like rabbits – the tropics do that to people. Once they're back in Holland, they'll pretend it never happened and join the congregation with prim faces listening to the pastor's sermons on Sunday morning'.

So she came back again and again, and it was great. But then, one evening, while having a beer with Alistair, he told me, 'Watch it, Bart, you're playing with fire.' He was right.

That shithead Werner sent a spy out, and when he had proof of my affair with the boss's wife, he ratted on me. I was fired on the spot. At least I was paid my dues, but it was made clear to me that nobody would hire me, and I might as well leave the country, which is what I did. Jeanette looked at me with complete disdain when I was leaving, as if nothing ever had happened. She had her eyes out already for the next stud."

"Where did you go?" Harry asked.

"I'll tell you," Bart responded.

7

A group of boys were playing soccer on the field some fifty yards in front of them when one accidentally kicked the ball in the bench's direction. Bart stood up, wanting to kick the ball back, but he was way off target, and the ball disappeared among the rhododendrons. Harry laughed,

"Sea legs are no soccer legs, Bart, you missed again, just like that rock you threw at the dragon."

"I know," Bart said, a bit embarrassed, but I can still kick your butt, buddy, and I won't miss."

They both laughed. One of the boys retrieved the ball from under the dense bushes, and then he smiled at the old men.

"Australia," said the failed soccer veteran when he sat down again. "I took a ferry boat to Sydney. She was a lovely ship, fast too, and I told the captain I was a sailor and asked if I could work on the ferry by any chance. He laughed. 'Not a chance in hell, mate,' he said in his Australian brawl, 'I have two officers, and that's two too many. The others are Indonesian deckhands'. So, I figured that my next job was probably going to be somewhere on shore again. The harbour in Sydney is just a harbour, and I have little to say about it except that opera building resembling a four master under sail. I wasn't going to spend my money on a hotel room, so I signed in at a seaman's boarding house in the harbour. Once I showed my ID proving I was a sailor, I could sleep there for two and a half bucks a night, with breakfast.

On the third day, when I went for a walk, I spotted a poster asking for men who could shoot rabbits – guns and shells supplied, generous pay, it read. So I went to the address listed, where two roughnecks asked some questions, wanted to see my papers, asked why I came to Australia and things. 'Why did you leave your job in Java?' they asked. I told them that I was fired and that I didn't care because it turned out to be a *fucking job* anyway, but only I saw the humour of that.

'Why were you fired, mate?' one of them, a big man with a bushy red beard and a dusty Akubra hat on his outback-weathered head, wanted to know. I thought about it for a moment, then said, 'For screwing the boss's wife'. They looked at me, then at each other and broke out into a burst of loud belly laughter.

'You know how to shoot a gun, Dutchy?' one said. 'Sure,' I answered. 'In that case, you're hired. Get your ass here tomorrow morning at seven, and we'll take you to the fields. Sign here.' He shoved a piece of paper across the table that was basically a document telling me they were not responsible for accidents. 'The pay is ten cents per rabbit, what? How's that supposed to be generous pay?' I asked. 'You'll see, sailor; you'll be smiling all the way to the bank.'

The next morning at seven, four other guys and I were loaded into the back of a red-dusted old Mac truck. One guy was from Tasmania, two others from Brisbane in Australia and one from England. I was curious, so I asked, 'Have any of you done this before?' 'I have', the Englishman said. 'So, what is it like?' I asked. 'Like a bloody avalanche of furry fuckers right in your face, and as far as you can see, you're shooting till your shoulder is pulverised. And then, you build a big heap of the critters, pour gasoline over it and bingo, your barbeque is cooking.'

'Then how the hell do they keep track of how many you shoot?' one of the Aussies asked. 'They don't,' the Brit said, 'but you're being paid well because they are.'

Once we left the city behind us, we were thrown about in the back of that bloody truck. We passed green pastures with thousands of sheep they call jumbucks. But we also went by areas with red dusty roads and fields. That dust would stick in your hair, on your face, in your ears and all over your clothes. We had to put a handkerchief over our mouth and nose not to suffocate. Then suddenly, the truck stopped in a valley, we rubbed the dust from our faces, and right in front of us were thousands, no, millions, of hopping bunnies. There was not a single spot without them. 'Holy mother of Jesus', one guy said, 'what the hell happened?' although that was not too difficult to answer. It was, however, more difficult to stop the multiplication. But how do you stop rabbits from being rabbits?

The beard jumped out of the truck cabin. 'Here, mates!' he

shouted. 'Come take your guns and ear covers. There is a rucksack for each of you with shells. Line up with some twenty yards distance between y'all, then start shooting and walking. Nothing else, shoot and walk. Don't bother about the ones you kill; we'll take care of that later. When your shells are gone, turn around facing this way, then we'll bring you a fresh supply. There is water in your rucksack.'

I checked my Beretta; it was an over and under in good condition. I loaded my pockets with shells and lined up on the extreme right wing, so I had no one on my starboard side.

We started to fire. It sounded like a bloody war, every shell was at least one rabbit, but it didn't seem to make a difference. No matter how many we shot, others kept jumping over the dead ones, and we could hardly walk forward. In less than two hours, my rucksack was empty. I turned around for a refill, and that's when I heard the same shooting a bit further on the left of us.

There was a rabbit plague in that part of Australia. Many villages were completely overrun by the furry creatures who not only destroyed gardens and devastated crops but also got into houses by the hundreds. We each shot thousands that day, and it did not seem to have even the slightest effect. Of course, this was a potential disaster, but there was no other immediate solution than just shooting them. I now realized that at ten cents apiece, we would indeed be generously paid.

When it was time to eat, the Aussies produced a Billypot, made a fire from dried wood, skinned a few of the rabbits we shot, put a splash of beer, spices and onions in the pot and we had lunch. I could not get it down my throat with those heaps of dead rabbits surrounding me. Also, my shoulder hurt like hell. They gave us some pieces of material we could wrap around our shoulders, but a fresh rabbit skin helped better. However, after three days, I gave up. I was badly bruised.

I could not lift my right arm anymore and even just breathing hurt like hell, so I went back to the city with the next transport. I must say, they kept their word, I was indeed very well paid, but it was no way for me to make money. I missed the sea.

Later I read that the shooting did not do enough to get rid of the bunnies, so they were poisoned with something that blinded them. Of course, shooting them was the more humane solution, but not effective enough.

Nevertheless, I made good money in Australia. Not by shooting rabbits but by finding gold.

I met a guy called Donald in a pub on a Saturday night when my arm was healed enough to lift a pint. We got to talk, and he seemed to be a nice guy. He'd just left the Australian army and planned to file a claim for a gold concession in the outback. I never realized there was gold in that country, but there is.

'Wanna join me?' Donald suggested. *Why not?* I thought. *Anything is better than shooting rabbits.*

Looking for gold in Australia is easy. All you need is a good metal detector, some other stuff and a lot of patience. If you're on crownland and you find gold, it's yours as long as you don't start a commercial mining operation; then you need licenses, and you pay tax.

The next day we went to a store called R.M.Williams, where you can buy everything you need. All the right clothes, Akubra hats, field shoes, tents, camping stuff, water containers, dried and canned food, everything – especially metal detectors and some hand tools you need for digging. We also bought two cheap shotguns and shells for protection. There was not much of my money left and not much of Donald's either, but we were ready to go and high-fived each other.

Donald had an old but well equipped Landrover, so we loaded our stuff onto the roof rack. We filled five jerrycans with gas, and two containers with water, bought more non-perishable groceries, then started our trip to a place called Kalgoorlie in West Australia, where gold was commercially mined. Despite being part of the 'Golden Mile' since the late 1890s, there was still enough crownland space for amateur prospectors to practice their hobby. Some of those hobbyists would sometimes find big nuggets worth a fortune."

"Did you?" Harry asked.

"Did I what?"

"Well, did you find a lot of gold? Did you get rich?"

A secretive smile appeared on Bart's face; he did not respond immediately. Instead, he took a moment before he nodded slowly, "I sure did, but it is only part of the story".

"My father worked in construction", Harry offered when Bart

did not continue his tales right away. "He did not have a profession like a carpenter, bricklayer or something. He was just a jack-of-all-trades. But he was an honest, hardworking father and husband who faithfully brought his meagre pay home each Saturday. Many a workman had to face a crying, livid desperate wife in those days because most of his week's pay went to the pub owner, and she would again not know how to feed the children. Alcoholism was rampant because life was miserable for many exploited lowly paid labourers working long hours and six-day weeks. There was no other entertainment for them than the pub and making babies, perpetuating their misery. On any given Saturday at the gate of a building site, one could find mothers with young children hoping to catch their husband and his pay before the pub owner did, who also waited at the gate. The pub owner usually won.

That was, of course, before there was a union that gradually improved the workers' situation.

Mother was born in Volendam; her whole life, she would wear the traditional Dutch costume, even while working at the market where she sold flowers. Maybe that's where my interest in the parks came from. I had two brothers and three sisters. We were not really poor, but there were no extras, and my parents never went on a vacation, not once in their whole life.

My sisters were very pretty, tall for girls, and many a guy's head in our poor neighbourhood would turn when they passed. My oldest sister became a nun, believe it or not. She wanted to become a missionary nun somewhere in Africa. Being poor and pretty can be a curse sometimes; it certainly was for my two younger sisters."

Harry's gaze followed two youthful women who, arm in arm, walked the park, laughing at something, enjoying the breezy spring day. He probably thought about his siblings, also once young and innocent so many years ago.

"They ended up in the red-light district of Amsterdam. My parents were devastated, but what could they do? Once those young women are in the grip of those goddamn pimps, parents have no chance. Of course, my mother did not want to face the shame in the neighbourhood anymore, so we moved to Amstelveen, outside the city. My father became depressed and withdrew in himself, and he stopped talking as much as he used to. He had been a God-fearing, honest man his whole life, working hard to support his family, and now two of his daughters were prostitutes, whores. It killed him, and it actually did because he died of heart failure. My brother went to the colonies like you, and my mother moved back to Volendam, where she lived with a sister, but then I was married already."

Harry went silent, so Bart decided to pick up his story again.

"From Sydney to Kalgoorlie is just over 2100 miles. Donald decided to take the highway to Adelaide, and from there, the coastal road to Perth rather than going through the outback and the dusty roads. We stopped halfway at some roadside tavern outside of Ceduna, where we had a good meal and an awful bed, so we were just as tired as the night before when we continued the following morning. But we were looking forward to the adventure, so that gave us energy. I insisted on driving the next stretch; it needed my constant attention. Not because of wallabies crossing the road – although they did – but because the nutcases there drive on the wrong side of the road!

We had another long day ahead of us as Kalgoorlie is about 370 miles east northeast of Perth.

We arrived at dawn in Boulder at the iconic Broken Hill Hotel, where we decided to stay for the night. We thought we'd have a good rest and shower before we went to the gold fields; not to mention, in Boulder, we could purchase some of the things we thought we still would need.

The whole area is known as the Goldfields, where fortunes are made and lost. You can even visit a museum where you can see copies of enormous nuggets that were found there. However, nobody tells you of just how many people spent everything they had to outfit themselves, yet never had a significant find and went back to their hometowns poorer than when they arrived.

Of course, old hands can spot greenhorns from a mile away and often try to take advantage of them. When we stepped out of the hotel in the morning, we were approached by a man offering us two nuggets the size of dove eggs. He needed cash, he claimed and would sell them to us for half price. Fortunately, we were forewarned about these crooks. What they offer looks very much like gold, but it is worthless. Another swindler offered us a hand-drawn map of a location next to where his own grandfather supposedly found a fortune in gold. Nobody ever worked that area, he claimed, and for a thousand bucks, it was ours. Of course, we decided to test our luck without the precious map."

Bart reclined, stretching his back, folding both hands behind his head, turning his face to the sun in its zenith now. More people were finding a spot on the grass, spreading a coat or a shawl, eating their lunch sandwiches – office workers escaping the concrete jungle for an hour. Two policemen on bicycles passed, slowly peddling, greeting the two seniors. Somewhere, somebody was playing a guitar.

Bart regained his hussar's position again.

"Searching for gold is actually easy. You just hold the metal detector coil an inch above the ground, moving it from left to right and back, just as a farmer mows the grass. You're wearing an earpiece covering both ears, attached to the coil with an electric wire. If there is metal in the ground, even a foot deep, the detector starts to beep – even if it's a tiny piece. And the closer to the metal, the louder it beeps."

Bart stood up, walking slowly, step by step, using his cane with both hands in front of him, making sweeping movements, left-right, left-right, demonstrating the use of a metal detector. Two young guys were passing on bicycles. One of them shouted over his shoulder, 'Hé grandpa, if you want to cut grass, it's over there,' and he pointed to the grass field in front of the rhododendrons.

"It's rather fun", Bart continued after sitting down again and parking his magic cane against the side of the bench. "Unless you really have to find gold because you need the money to pay for all the expenses you accrued travelling, lodging, outfitting etc., because then you usually find shit and end up on the street peddling fake gold or treasure maps.

It took us quite a while to find a spot where we could try our luck. The whole area is given out as a concession to companies or individuals who staked their claims, so you can't do anything there. We ended up driving northwest on salt flats until we found an area that was still government property, where anybody who was crazy enough to try in that godforsaken hell was welcome.

We set up camp at a spot where some brush and a few eucalyptus trees were growing on the edge of a stretch of dry grass, thorny thistles and a kind of prickly cacti. All around us, as far as we could see, it was desert, comprising of large white patches from the dried salt, with some growth and lots of rocks and gravel amongst dusty red sand. There were many signs that somebody or something had been digging small shallow holes all over, so we were certainly not the first trying our luck there.

'I stopped here, Bart,' Donald said, 'because look, from here to far in the distance, it looks like a sort of meandering valley with patches of vegetation like this spot here. I assume that the branch of an old river may have flown here – one that dried out ages ago.' I could see his point, but I said, 'don't you think that people before us could have come to that same conclusion?'

'I'm sure they did, and like you, they may have concluded that, therefore that area is worked over many times. But I like to test my luck, buddy. I suggest we work together; you take the left side, I'll take the right. Make sure you cover your half completely, don't hurry, you might be missing a good find, we share fifty-fifty. Try your detector. Does it work?'

I threw my pocketknife on the ground, passed over it with the coil and immediately heard a loud beeping. 'OK, we're set, now watch out for the snakes here; they're deadly', Donald warned me. So off we went, and in all honesty, I was very excited. *Fuck* I thought, *I'm a gold prospector.*

We walked till the sun was right above our head, burning like hell, and I was sweating like a draft-horse in summer. There had only been two beeps on my side, a nail and a rusted part of a sardine can. We walked back to camp to rest a bit in the shade; Donald had found nothing either. 'What do you think?' I asked him. He just smiled while leaning against a trunk, 'Nothing, man, this is nothing. If it was so easy to find something, don't you think the entire bleeding country would be here?' I had to agree.

We continued where we had stopped, about fifty meters from camp. Not even twenty minutes later, Donald shouted 'BINGO' and indicated that I should come over. He moved his metal detector over a particular spot, and it kept singing an undulating meow like a tomcat in heat. Donald started digging carefully with a small shovel, throwing the dirt on top of the screaming coil. There was a handful of sand and sandy pebbles, Donald picked up one of them, and the frenetic beeping stopped. He cleaned the detector coil of the dirt, put the pebble back on it, and the racket started again. Beaming a big smile at me, Donald retrieved a small bottle of water from his breast pocket and washed the pebble with it. Suddenly it turned a shiny yellow. He held it in the palm of his hand, letting the sun reflect from it. 'This, my friend', he said triumphantly, 'is what a one-ounce nugget looks like'.

That's when gold fever hit me.

'Holy mother Maria', I said, intuitively forgetting my sailor's curses, faced with this solemn moment. 'So you were right, my friend, let's see if there is more.' I was already sweeping my detector. That afternoon Donald found three more nuggets. Two were smaller than the first find, and the other a bit bigger; he also found several tiny pieces. I added a rusted screwdriver without a handle to our fortune. However, just before dawn, I picked up a rock over which my detector kept screaming, but it looked just like a dirty rock, the size of half a tennis ball. It had an odd shape for a pebble, and I was about to throw it aside when I thought better. 'Donald', I shouted, 'have a look at this.'

When Donald walked over and saw the rock, he grabbed both my elbows and started dancing around.' Holy shit Bart', he laughed, 'your first time, and you find a big fucking nugget worth more than my fucking car.' Anyway, what can I say? Donald had been damn right. Most amateur prospectors must have thought the valley had been worked over too much, but apparently not with our sophisticated tools. So for the next couple of weeks, we kept finding nuggets, all the same size as Donald found the first day. Then on the second day of the third week, our provisions were almost gone, and the water wouldn't last two more days. I even almost stepped on a snake, the exact same colour as the hot sand – I never saw the damned serpent, but luckily it slithered away. 'Give thanks to your maker, buddy', Donald said. 'A bite from that one, and within a couple of hours, you'd have been dancing the polka with your great-grandparents above.'

I was still shaking, but for some odd, inexplicable reason, I decided to check the exact spot where that serpent had been lying. Believe it or not, my detector screamed like a hungry piglet.

'Donald', I shouted, 'come have a look here.'

Yes, it was a nugget, but what kind of nugget? It resembled a big piece of driftwood when we finally unearthed the whole thing, and it was heavy as hell. Donald, who had been dancing when I found my first nugget, was just sitting there, staring at the unbelievable find. When he finally found his voice, he said, 'Dutchy, my friend, you're looking at a million bucks right there.' Then it was my turn to lose my voice.

It took both of us to carry the enormous lump to our camp. Fortunately, there were no witnesses.

When we put everything together, the other nuggets appearing small and irrelevant compared to the huge one, we decided to go back to Kalgoorlie the next day, but not to check-in at the hotel. We would have a good night's sleep right here, then, taking turns, drive back to Sydney without stopping. It was Donald's smart thinking that we did not lose every single ounce we found.

He insisted against my objections to take our tent down, bury the big lump in the sand, then erect the tent over it again. So our treasure was now hidden in the centre of our tent, under the floor canvas. Although Donald had a leather pouch that held a few other nuggets."

Harry was listening breathlessly. He had no perception of a million; it was just a word to him very seldom used in his circles. At best, he knew that a guy named Rockefeller was a millionaire, as was the queen, but for people like Harry, who seldom even saw a hundred, it was as abstract as the hereafter. To just *find* a million was so incomprehensible to him that he just stared and didn't even bother to ask questions.

"We were just sitting in front of our tent sharing our last lukewarm beer when I spotted a dust cloud in the distance that quickly moved in our direction. We were on our guard. The dust cloud stopped some thirty yards left of our tent, revealing a rust bucket of a truck; three ruffians jumped out of it. Slowly walking towards us, like John Wayne in the movies, they stopped in front of us. 'G'day mate', the tallest one greeted us,' had any luck here?' But Donald was not going to be stupid. 'Been better, mate', he answered, but the guy kept his gaze on him. He then flashed his rotten teeth at Donald with a grin, spat on the ground, and said, 'Is that so? Then maybe you shitheads don't mind showing us how bad, bad is, eh?' He drew a revolver, slowly pointing it at our faces. This was serious trouble. It was only then that I realized just how smart Donald had been.

'Why would I do that?' Donald said. 'Well, cause maybe you want to pay for something, mate.'

'What would I want to pay for?' Donald asked, playing like he was stupid.

'Your fucking lives, mate', the gangster said, all the time smiling like a friendly crocodile.

'Go ahead, check the tent', Donald said, holding his hands above his head. The gunman signalled to his cronies, who went through our stuff, came out with our guns and shells and said, 'Nothing, boss.'

The boss body-searched me first but found nothing, of course. Then he checked Donald and found the leather pouch. He looked inside and smiled victoriously, 'Well, mate', he said, 'your bad is good enough for us. I forgot to introduce meself, I'm the tax collector, and these are my helpers.' He roared with laughter, pocketed the purse, jumped back in the truck as did his accomplices and disappeared in a cloud of dust. Donald screamed and cursed, waving his fist until they were out of sight, then he almost died laughing. 'That went well,' he said, 'now let's get the hell out of here.'

It did not take us long, with our treasure rolled up in a tarp between the seats behind us, to be on our way. The robbery at gunpoint indicated that the sooner we would be leaving the Goldfields, the better. 'Now what, Donald?' I asked my friend, 'How do we turn that big lump into a million bucks?' I don't know exactly, Bart, give me some time to think,' he answered.

By the time we were back in Sydney, at around eleven in the morning of the following day, he knew. We stopped in front of a downtown office building with a brass plate engraved with **Townsend & Perlbaum**, *Attorneys at Law*. 'Bart, you stay in the car; I'll be back soon. This is an old friend of my father. He'll know how to handle this', Donald said.

Twenty minutes later, we followed Mr Townsend to the CBA, The Commonwealth Bank of Australia. I stayed in the car again, but they both came back with a third gentleman a quarter of an hour later. 'Mr Townsend, this is my friend Bart', Donald said, and we shook hands, then the lawyer introduced me to a Mr Breeman, who was the bank manager. Donald and I carried the nugget still wrapped in the tarp inside the building. Quite a few employees were throwing funny looks at us. We were still unshaven and in our dusty gold-digging outfits, not exactly the kind of clients the boss would generally bother with. Finally, the group plus another bank official walked to the safe, and it took both the boss and the official to open the ten-inch-thick steel door. We deposited the nugget on the floor, then took off the tarp, and Mr Townsend took a picture with his camera.

We were then taken to a meeting room, where Donald and I opened a bank account in the presence of the lawyer. Thank God I still carried my passport! Naturally, Donald didn't, but Mr Townsend vouched for him."

"So now you had half a million bucks?" Harry asked, looking as if he'd just won the national lottery himself.

"No, not yet", Bart answered. "You know, gold has a certain official price. But nuggets, particularly very special ones like the one I found, are usually auctioned off at a much higher price per troy ounce – that's what they call it. So Donald and Mr Townsend would take care of that, and when it was sold, half the money would be booked into my account. But the bank manager asked if I needed some cash right away, and when I said 'yes, please', he gave me ten thousand bucks.

I checked into the Hilton because now I had money enough, but they sure looked suspicious at the check-in desk when I paid down a cash deposit, looking like a bum. However, the next day I bought some clothes, had a shave and a haircut and then they smiled warmly at me.

Within a week, the nugget was sold to a casino in Las Vegas, America, for one point six million. So then there was eight hundred thousand in my account, can you believe that?"

"Did you go back to find more gold? Harry wanted to know.

"No, not me mister. I was more than satisfied with that much money in my account. Plus, I still remembered the poisonous serpent that almost got me, not to mention those hoodlums that could have robbed and killed us."

"So, what did you do?" Harry reached into the inside pocket of the coat that he had folded over the back of the bench and withdrew a brown paperback, from which he produced a rye bread sandwich. "Would you like half?" He held it out to Bart, who looked at the offering as if to determine whether it met his gourmet standards but reached out and bit into it with gusto.

"I found money too," Harry divulged while chomping on his lunch, moving a bit closer to Bart as if it was still a secret. "Not as much as you, of course, and I didn't keep it at first, let me tell you."

He stood up from the bench to throw the crumpled paper bag in the trash bin across the path, then sat down, hesitating for a few seconds as if to determine how to formulate his story.

8

"Anna was still alive, and the kids were little. I was still in planting. I bought a good second-hand bicycle for my wife, so she didn't have to walk to her work each day. I needed some working clothes, Manchester pants, a jacket, and high boots, so we would be pretty short for a few weeks, but that was OK. My darling could squeeze a buck into six quarters.

It was a Monday morning, and I was early in the park, always was. That's why the park later promoted me to maintenance, I think. We were going to work on the gladiolus, which means you have to walk past the lilac bushes over there in front of those chestnuts. Now, mind you, as I said, it was Monday morning. That spot between the chestnuts and the lilacs was a favourite spot for lovers who went to the park to do more than just hold hands or stare into each other's eyes, if you know what I mean, especially during the weekend. It was as if my eyes were drawn to the shiny brown rectangular object in the grass. I picked it up, and guess what? It was a thick leather billfold. I had a quick look, and there was a stash of cash in it. I put it in the inside pocket of my jacket, but the whole day I was curious, and when it was finally five o'clock, I hurried home.

I showed Anna what I found, and we emptied it on the table, precisely two thousand three hundred and fifty guilders – almost as much as I made in a whole year. There was also a picture of a woman, club membership cards, a driving licence, and three business cards. One had the same name as the driving licence, so that must have been the owner.

Benno van Staveren

The Windmill Trading Comp. Ltd

Chief Executive Officer

Merwedelaan 26 ------- Tel: 082- 44 120.

Of course, there was not a single moment that we thought of keeping the money; we were poor but honest people. But we knew that if you found money, you sort of were entitled to a ten percent finders-fee. And two hundred and thirty guilders would be like a fortune for us then.

The next day I asked if I could leave my job an hour early, and because I never asked, it was not a problem. So I went home, washed and changed into my Sunday clothing, and then took line 6 to the exclusive river neighbourhood with expensive mansions and shiny cars in front. With the billfold in my hand, I climbed the five granite stairs and rang the bell. I could hear it chiming hollow through a long corridor or a large hallway, then footsteps approached, and the door half-opened. 'Yes?' a woman said. I felt she was not the lady of the house, 'I would like to speak to Mr van Staveren' I responded, hiding the reason for my visit behind my back.

'Wanda, who is that?' a chic female voice sounded from somewhere deep inside the house.

'A man for mister, madam', Wanda answered.

'Then don't let him stand outside. Bring the gentleman into the library; I will be there in a second.'

I followed Wanda to a room in the front of the house that had many books against the wall and a big table with six chairs in the centre. 'Please sit down', said Wanda, who was now a bit more friendly than when she'd opened the door. She left the room. I was sitting there on the edge of my chair. I could look out of the tall windows to the street and see the canal with tourist boats going in both directions. One window was slightly open; I could hear birds singing in the lime trees already in full bloom along the water's edge, and the Westertoren chimed in the distance. As it happened, the lady's second turned out to be twenty minutes, but then a charming woman opened the door, with both hands still trying to fix an earring in place while she approached, she said, 'Good morning, sorry for making you wait. What can I help you with, Mr eh...'

I stood up, 'Vilder', I said, 'Harry Vilder, madam, and I was actually looking for Mr van Staveren.' 'I see', she said, 'but my husband is not home right now, If it is personal, you may have to come back at about six o'clock, but can I tell him what you want to see him for?'

'Eh, oh yes, sure, madam, I found your husband's billfold, madam.'

'You did?'

'Yes, madam, and luckily your husband's card was in it, so I knew to whom it belonged.'

'Where did you find it, Mr Vilder? I was shopping with my husband in the P.C.Hooft on Saturday morning, and I am sure he still had it then.' Mrs van Staveren seemed to be surprised.

'In the Vondelpark madam, I am the head of maintenance, and when I walked to the gladiolus yesterday morning, I found this in the grass behind the lilac bushes.'

Mrs van Staveren said nothing. Her face turned white; she tightened her lips and stood up from her chair, all the while keeping her eyes on the brown billfold on the table in front of the stranger before her, as if at any second it could explode.

'So, do I understand that you work in the park every day, Mr Vilder?'

'Yes, madam, I do.'

'And this spot where you said you found my husband's billfold, what kind of a part of the park would you say it is.?"

'They call it Lovers Lane, mam'. I blabbered it out before I realized it. The blood started rising to my face. 'Not exactly there, but close by it, madam'. I tried, but she never bought it.

Alfred Balm

'Let me have a look', she said, then emptied the billfold on the table. All the money came out,

the driving licence, club cards and business card, and also the photo of the woman. I immediately noticed that the woman in the photograph was not Mrs van Staveren, and so did she.

'The cheating bastard', she hissed like a viper, her eyes shooting fire.

'Mr Vilder', she said with great self-control, 'thank you for your honesty, you won't regret it. It may not surprise you that my husband is in for a lot of trouble tonight. Please be so kind as to wait here, maybe half an hour or so, until he comes home. Can you do that?' She put everything back in the billfold then placed it again in front of me on the table. 'I would appreciate it if you forget what happened just now and pretend you just arrived to hand my husband his billfold.' she asked.

What choice did I have? So I said, 'Of course madam..'

I was sitting there in that quasi bookshop for almost half an hour, nervous like hell, when there was a noise in the hallway, a sort of *Honey I'm Home* tumult. Then I heard the voice of Mrs van Staveren. 'There is somebody waiting for you in the library', she said.

I could hear a bit of conversation in hushed voices, and then a gentleman entered, I would say about fifty years old, a well-dressed man, his black hair greying above his ears. There was a surprised expression on his face. He looked at me as if he smelled dogshit. His gaze fell immediately on his billfold; he looked at my face, at the billfold again, then said in an aggressive voice, 'Where the hell did you get that?' But he changed immediately when Mrs van Staveren entered."

Bart hadn't been very interested at first in Harry's stories, too domestic for the adventurer's taste, but now he moved a bit closer and pricked up his ears. He smelled a spicy one.

"What happened then?" he asked when Harry did not immediately continue his narrative.

"Mr van Staveren became very agitated; his face was as white as his shirt. 'Where the hell did you do that, you damned thief? How did you pick my pocket without me noticing? You know they do that all the time darling, look at his clothes, his dirty hands. He's just a labourer, a bum, stealing my wallet then asking for a finder's fee.' Then turning to me, he said, 'Isn't that so? You despicable low-life. I hope you didn't pay him something, hon?'

'Mr Vilder, can you please tell my husband where and when you found that thing?' his wife asked me. Mr van Staveren reached for his billfold, but she was just a bit quicker. 'I'll hold on to this for now', she said.

'I didn't take anything, honestly', I started, 'it is all there, all two thousand three hundred and fifty guilders, sir. I just looked to find out who lost it there.'

'Tell us where, please', Mrs van Staveren repeated.

'I found it in the park, the Vondelpark where I am head of maintenance, on Monday morning behind the lilac bushes on the grass.'

'Is there a particular name for that area, Mr Vilder?' she asked, but now I knew why. I hesitated.

'Well?' she insisted.

'Lovers Lane, mam, they call it Lovers Lane.'

Mr van Staveren lost the last bit of his dignity. He looked like he just crapped his pants. His lips began twisting, he kept his gaze in despair on the face of his wife, without speaking a word, then in a thin voice he pleaded,

'Don't believe him, darling, it is a trick, or maybe somebody stole my billfold and lost it there.'

At that point, his wife emanating utter disgust, emptied the wallet on the table, shoving the wad of guilders in my direction. 'Yes, you disgusting philanderer and the thief also put this picture in it'. She held the photo of the woman in front of his face. 'Have a good look at your whore, because that is all you are going to see from now on. You'll be hearing from my lawyer, Don Juan Dickhead.'

The man seemed to shrink before her eyes.

'Mr Vilder, please take that money, it's yours'. She turned to address her shrunken husband. 'And you, you arrogant dirtbag, have a good look at this labourer, this bum as you dare call an honest man, because he is more of a gentleman than you'll ever be.'

I was glad when she called for Wanda to show me out.

Anna was over the moon when I showed her the money and told her the story. It solved all our problems. 'Lovers Lane, eh?' she quipped, 'don't let me ever get you behind the lilacs, mister."

76

Harry retrieved a large handkerchief from his pocket. After loudly blowing his nose, he critically inspected the harvest as a fortune teller reading tea leaves. He then folded it up and put it back in his pocket.

9

"Life wasn't any different at first," said Bart, "it just felt different. It felt like strangers in the street, people in shops or at the hotel seemed to know – *there goes a guy with eight hundred thousand dollars in the bank*. But that was, of course, nonsense. It is true that it feels strange when you suddenly don't have to care about money anymore, when you can buy something without wondering how the hell you're going to pay for it. I told you already that I wasn't going to try my luck prospecting for gold again, so now there wasn't a real reason to stay in Australia. My money was safe in a reputable bank, and I could transfer from it to any place in the world.

I figured I had been a landlubber long enough; the sea was calling. But I was not gonna be a sailor again, no sir, not Bart Bouman anymore. I was gonna buy myself a boat.

So I said goodbye to Donald, who, as it happens, went to England, and I booked myself a ticket to the island of Curacao, travelling through Amsterdam. I stayed a couple of days in Hotel American, which, as you know, is within walking distance from where we are sitting now.

After having been away, the old city looked different, and it didn't feel like home anymore. Maybe because it rained every day, or maybe because I lived like a damned tourist in a hotel, I don't know. Still, I was glad when I finally went to Schiphol airport and boarded my KLM flight to Willemstad, which is the capital of that Caribbean island.

I flew first class. Man, what an experience! You're treated like royalty by the nice stewardesses, *'Would you like a glass of champagne, Mr Bouman? Here is the menu, Mr Bouman. Would you like a blanket Mr Bouman?'* I loved every minute of it. Did you ever fly?"

"Me?" Harry answered, "Yes once, there was a fair on the Dam square; we had a day off because it was the Queen's birthday. The day before, we made a huge crown of orange Tagetes, marigolds, you would call them, on the grass there in the centre. Anyway, I took Hanna, who was still little, to the fair. There was a tremendous carousel, and she wanted to go in it but not alone. 'Daddy, you gotta come with me, daddy, come with me!' So there I was, sitting in a small airplane hanging on four chains turning round and round, feeling like an idiot flying high over the heads of the crowd, with the music blaring way too loud. While still flying, my little daughter next to me suddenly vomited, spraying the contains of her stomach in a wide circle across the panicking bystanders running for cover just in time.

That was my only experience in a plane, and I didn't like it."

Bart laughed. "Yes, I wouldn't call that first class, but seriously, flying is great, man. You can't imagine how this whole building, with many people drinking coffee, having dinner, reading a paper or just napping, can stay in the air. And you know something? You never feel the speed even though it goes ten times faster than a train, or maybe even faster, I don't know.

Anyway, I fell asleep when they turned out the lights, and I only woke up when they switched them on again. I was hungry by that time, so I was glad when a big breakfast comprising coffee, hot rolls, scrambled eggs, bacon, baked potatoes, and fresh orange juice was served.

About an hour later, the captain said we were going to land on Hato, the airport of Curacao and '*thank you for flying KLM*' and '*it's a delightful thirty degrees Celsius here.*'

I had not booked a hotel yet, but that appeared to be no problem. Curacao is a relatively small island and very colourful. The tiny Dutch-style houses are painted in many different pastel colours, and the people come in all shades from white to black and many brown shades in between.

I took a taxi to the Avila Beach Hotel, the oldest hotel there. To get there, you have to cross the harbour across a bridge that is floating on a whole string of boats. The cab driver was very talkative, trying to extract more out of the newcomer than just a taxi fare. He highly recommended a place called Campo Alegre or something, but I was not interested in tourist attractions, so I said 'no thanks.' Later I learned that it is a place with only prostitutes, and it is big business for cab drivers to take clients there.

I had planned to stay for quite some time in Curacao, but I left after only three days. Not that it isn't a nice Island, it is charming, but not for what I had in mind.

So I flew to Nassau, the capital of the Bahamas, situated on New Providence Island."

"Why did you do that? Is it bigger or nicer?" Harry asked.

"No, that wasn't it. My plan was to buy a nice fishing boat, one that I could go fishing on myself, but could also be chartered out to tourists, so she would pay for herself. I was told the Bahamas was the place for that. Curacao was more of a tourist destination.

I found out that there were many good banks there, Bank of America, J.P.Morgan, Bank of Canada and several local banks, so I knew it wouldn't be a problem to transfer money from Sydney to the Bahamas. I checked into the Beach Hotel, then right away walked to the harbour where many nice fishing boats were moored. Most of them were for charter, but quite a few had a *For Sale* sign.

The next thing I did was open an account with J.P Morgan and transfer a hundred thousand dollars from Australia. The account manager was a friendly young Bahamian guy who asked me why I came to his island. I explained to him that I intended to buy a fishing boat – not a new one, but a good used one – then live on the island for a while, go fishing, charter the boat out and enjoy life. I apparently hit it off with Ronaldo – that was the guy's name – because he invited me for a drink at six that evening. We went to a bar with a nice terrace under palm trees, overlooking the ocean. He introduced me to a special Bahamian cocktail with rum. They served something called conch fritters, which is a local delicacy. You know those big snail shells that are pink inside? That's them."

"You mean they're eating big snails there? You didn't do that too, did you?" Harry almost gagged at the thought.

"Sure I did, and it's actually quite good, spicy but tasty. Then while we were sitting on the terrace, having a few more drinks and watching the sunset, Ronaldo suddenly said, 'Hey Bart, I just thought of something. There's a great fishing boat, a *Hatteras Carolina*, nearly two and a half years old and very well maintained. It's owned by a Bahamian man who captains the boat himself. He is a very nice, decent sort of a guy; he has a family of six, built a house almost entirely with his own hands. We financed both the house and the boat. We should have foreclosed on him several times, but I could hold it off. He's an honest, hard-working man, but he just took on too much debt. So as it stands, we're about to take either his house or the boat. Would you be interested in having a look at the boat?'

The next day I went to the harbour to see the boat and meet the owner.

The boat appeared new on the outside, the paint was shiny, and everything was spic and span.

Overall, its length was about 65 feet, it had a great tower, and the twin Cat C-32A Diesel engines seemed to be in excellent condition. What was important to me was that the engine room was as clean as the kitchen of a five-star restaurant – it is the best indicator that the captain takes good care of his boat. The owner, who introduced himself as Hernando, was a sympathetic kind of a guy, maybe in his early fifties. He invited us on board, pointed to the basket where we could put our shoes, then showed us around. Whenever he walked the gangway, he would lightly rub the teak railing as if to move fingerprints. He offered us drinks which amazed me. After all, I was there to maybe buy his boat, taking away the means to make a living for his family.

When we sat down, I asked Ronaldo what the problem was. 'How much did Hernando owe the bank?' 'All in all, about seventy-five thousand dollars', Ronaldo said, 'and he is six months behind now.'

'You know I always paid Mr Ronaldo, each month, but we had that terrible storm, and the season was lost.' said Hernando. 'That is only partially correct, Hernando', answered Ronaldo, 'many of the other boats did well and paid their debt, you know how I tried to avoid the sale, but my hands are tied. The head office took over the file and now insists on foreclosure. I am sorry. You're a good man, and I hate to see what's happening to one of my fellow countrymen, one of the last few Bahamian boat owners, especially now it's almost only foreigners in the business'.

'How much did you pay for the boat when you bought her?' I asked Hernando.

'I had saved fifty thousand from running boats here, sir. The bank loaned me two hundred and fifty thousand with the *Estrella del Mar* as security, and I finally had my own boat. I was doing fine in the beginning, and I paid every month, and if I was not out fishing, I worked on the boat. I made her brand-new sir, as you can see, you being a sailor and things, I can tell sir. Once the sea is in your blood, it always shows, never lies.'

'Ronaldo, the money he still owes the bank, is that secured by the boat only or by his house as well?'

'I am afraid it is. We hold both as security against the outstanding amount and are ordered by head office to close on both.' He looked down at his hands, ashamed of being the spokesperson for some abstract authority somewhere abroad that could take a man's house and his business for being behind in paying back a loan.

'So Hernando, I said, how much would you say your *Estrella* is worth today?'

'After all the work I did and things I replaced? I'd say at least half a million bucks mon, maybe more.'

'You agree with that, Ronaldo?' I asked.

Ronaldo thought for a moment, then slowly nodded. 'Very possible, Bart, very possible.'

'So if you confiscate his boat and his house, his debt is settled, and the bank owns both? Excuse me for being ignorant; I'm not a banker, but suppose if you sell his boat and house for, say, four hundred thousand, do you then pay Hernando the three hundred thousand, assuming you take twenty-five thousand for your trouble?'

Ronaldo blushed and moved uncomfortably in his chair, 'I

wish Bart, I honestly wish, but that's not how it works. If the bank repossesses something they accepted as security, it's theirs, and the profit or loss is for the bank.'

Hernando, the captain owner of the boat, didn't move. He tried hard not to show any emotion, but his mouth twisted in his stoic brown face, and his dark eyes started tearing up.

I felt for the poor man who had obviously been a hard-working person falling on bad luck or who overextended himself being too optimistic about his prospects.

An idea started to take form in my brain.

'Hernando,' I said, 'I would like to meet your family. You think that is possible?'

I noticed a question on both faces, but Hernando's turned into a smile. 'Of course, sir, with pleasure', he answered. 'And by the way, captain, no more *sir*, just call me Bart. Seamen among seamen, remember?' I added.

The house was small but in perfect condition, freshly painted, and the small garden with a few banana and papaya trees was well attended to. On both sides of the sky-blue entrance door were large pots with pink bougainvillea climbing against the yellow wall. The door opened, and a broad smiling Bahamian mamma with a baby in her arms greeted her husband, then she extended her free hand to me. 'I am Flora, welcome, mister', and her smile seemed even wider. 'Come in, Bart!' Hernando invited me. 'The kids are all in school, but this one still has to suffer the terror of teacher mamma'.

As I expected, the house inside was as neat as the boat. The furniture was modern, and the decorations on the wall were pictures of snow-topped alps, windmills along a Dutch river and the Eiffel Tower in Paris. 'Please sit down,' Flora told me, 'Can I get you a drink, my husband doesn't drink, but I do have cold beer in the fridge, or orange juice, maybe?' I asked for the latter.

'Hernando, I may have a solution for your problem. Ronaldo is a nice man, but somewhere up high in that bank is a man without a soul, just looking at numbers instead of people, a damned shylock. You paid three hundred thousand for your boat. What if I pay seventy-five thousand to the bank and seventy-five thousand to you so you can get your life in order and have some money in your name again, but twenty-five thousand will be in a separate account as working capital? I am half owner together with you, you captain the boat, and we split 50/50?'

Hernando looked at me with an open mouth, not believing what he heard. One moment he thought he was going to lose everything, and the next, he saw a future again. Flora started crying, and the baby, sensing something wrong, joined her but did a much better job of it.

The next day we went to the bank together, sitting opposite Ronaldo's desk. Another gentleman was standing next to him, watching the two of us with mistrust; I didn't like him.

'Here's the deal, gentlemen', I said. 'I am willing to pay the seventy-five thousand dollars of Hernando's debt in full. In exchange, you release the security on his boat and his house.

We'll open a new joint account and deposit twenty-five

thousand dollars in it. *The Estrella del Mar* will be jointly owned by Hernando and me but operated by Hernando at his discretion.

If that meets with your approval, please prepare the documents, and we will be back here tomorrow to sign and transfer the money.' There was a look of surprise on the face of the asshole standing next to Ronaldo, who probably thought we came to beg but not to pay down the debt. I noticed a faint smile on Ronaldo's lips.

'That would be quite acceptable, sir,' said the asshole. 'Ronaldo, make sure the documents will be ready' he turned on his heels without saying goodbye."

"So, did you do that, Bart? That was a damn nice thing of you to do, you didn't even know that Hernando! So what happened next?" Harry didn't want to miss a word.

"Well, I was the co-owner of a sixty-footer, so whaddya think? I went fishing. Hernando used to have a deckhand who took care of the fishing gear when clients were on board. He would make sure that there was sufficient baitfish, put the fishing poles in the rocket launcher behind the fishing chair on the aft deck – that's what they call that thing – put the outriggers out, bait the hooks and keep an eye out to see if there are signs of fish, frigate birds for example, who can spot fish from way up high.

If there was a strike, Johny would set the hook, then shout 'FISH ON', and the client takes the rod then fights the catch.

Because of Hernando's financial trouble, Johny had been let go. He was very worried because he had become the father of a baby boy and then lost his job; that's tough. So he was over the moon when he got his job back and was assured of weekly pay again.

I liked Johny, he loved fishing, and that's very important if you take people out paying up to a few thousand dollars a day.

So we went out a few days after everything with the bank was settled. The weather was just right, with a few clouds and a ripple on the water. Hernando was running the boat from the tower as proud as a king, and Johny was busy baiting the rods. I was sitting on the aft deck, taking in a bit of sun, deeply inhaling the salty air of the sea, realizing how much I had missed it. We were about an hour out when the captain slowed the boat down to about eight knots, and Johny pointed at a couple of frigate birds circling above us, 'Watch it, mon", he shouted excitedly at me, I laughed at the familiarity. Suddenly one of the lines was pulled from the clip on the starboard outrigger, and the reel on one of the rods started singing. 'FISH ON'..screamed Johny, quite unnecessarily because I was already sitting in the fighting chair. Hernando stopped the boat, Johny handed me the rod, and I could feel from the pull that I had a big fish on. However, there was no way that I could reel it in, the fish kept taking line. 'LET IT GO, LET IT GO', shouted Hernando from above, then one of the other rods started shaking, and Johny grabbed it. Now we had two fish on and still two more lines out. That's when I found out that Hernando's deckhand was a professional. He did not panic at all. Instead, he calmly set the hook on the rod in his hand, tightened the slip on the reel a bit, took the rod on portside and reeled it in so fast that no fish went for it.

Then he did the same with the third rod, but he got a strike on it anyway. So now we had to fight three fish while trying to avoid the lines that would cross. Hernando hurried down from the top deck and took the centre rod, letting the fish take all the line it wanted. 'Dorado, Bart', he said, but I knew."

"What is Dorado?" Harry wanted to know, sitting tight, straightening his back, his hands together in front of him as if fighting the pull of some sea monster.

"A tasty fish, with green and blue colours like a parrot when in the water, but the colours soon disappear once the fish is landed. It's a great fighter that swims in schools, so if you catch one, you usually catch more, as we did that day.

Anyway, I knew the routine. I pulled the rod with all my might towards me. Then, reeling in as fast as I could, I pointed the tip towards the fish, pulled back again while not reeling, and repeated the procedure, bringing the fish with pumping movements towards the boat. It was a six-foot bull, who made a final effort to escape just when Johny was about to hook it. But I was ready, giving him all the line he wanted. He soon gave up, and I reeled him in. I landed the first fish on my own boat, and it sure was a keeper. Johny pulled in his fish next. It was still a nice one but a bit smaller. Then Hernando handed me the rod he was handling. The fish had taken virtually all the line, which was why our lines did not cross, and we did not lose a fish, but I had a hell of a time reeling it in. It was an unbelievable six inches bigger than the first one I caught.

We landed six more, and then I called it a day. My arm was sore, but I could still lift a cold beer and toast with the crew on a successful first trip, noticing the captain drank a Coca Cola. Then Hernando explained that there was an additional source of income. Johny made filets of the fish, packed them in plastic bags and within an hour after tying the boat to the cleats in the harbour, the fresh fish would be in the freezer of a local hotel. Did you ever fish?" Bart asked Harry.

10

"When Jaap was young, he always wanted to go fishing, but I didn't have much time for it, so I never went," Harry said. "But when he was 5 or 6, I bought him a fishing rod, nothing special, just a cheap short sort of thing, with a line and a bobber, and I filed the hook down so it wouldn't hurt him. Man, was he happy with it; he was the proudest boy you've ever seen. Every now and then, I would take Jaapie with me to the park. He could play a bit there while I kept an eye on him. He would help me with planting as kids do, you know, until he got bored, then I'd properly replant what he had done. In those days, we still had a pond on the east side with some fish in it. There were signs, *NO FISHING* and *NO SWIMMING*. But people would throw all sorts of stuff in it, and during summer, teenagers would sometimes skinny dip in it, so people started complaining, and we got rid of it. It was over there," Harry pointed, "where those glasshouses have been built now.

But when Jaapie was small, the pond was still there, and of course, the little boy wanted to fish with his brand-new rod, so I put a small piece of flower stem on the hook and said, 'Ok, go catch a big one, Jaapie.' I was working on the irises, so I was close to the water and could keep him in my sight. Now you must know that we used to have two city park wardens as well – thank God we don't anymore, but then we still did. They were pseudo cops with no authority whatsoever. Still, they decked themselves out with heavy belts, with flashlights, several leather pouches holding a compass, and binoculars or something in it, attached to the belt. On their shoulders, they had epaulettes with the city's crest, and they would be wearing heavy boots. They patrolled my park like it was their private domain. We hated them, especially one, a fanatical jerk with the IQ of a garden gnome and the charm of a cactus.

I was focused on my work when I suddenly heard Jaapie scream, 'Daddy, my fishing rod!' I was there in a split second; my little boy stood there bawling, and on the ground in front of him was his rod, broken in two. The jerk was standing next to him, triumphantly pointing to the *NO FISHING* sign. 'Did you do that?' I asked, hardly able to control myself picking up the pieces of the rod. 'Yes,' he said. 'No fishing is no fishing, and....' But whatever else he wanted to say, I don't know because I grabbed the back of his collar and pants and threw him face down in the pond. When he surfaced with mud and weeds all over his head and shoulders, he was much less impressive than he'd thought himself to be when he'd dressed for duty that morning. I pointed at the other sign and said, 'And NO SWIMMING is no swimming, either.' I felt much better and told Jaapie I would buy him a new rod, an even nicer one.

Three days later, I had to report to my supervisor and tell him what happened. I knew he had children himself, and he listened then smiled. 'Harry', he said, 'I think I would have done the same, but don't let it happen again. We should get rid of that pond anyway. It is nothing but trouble.'

So that was my only experience with fishing, Bart."

"At first", Bart mused, "I thought I could go the rest of my life doing nothing other than just spend my days in the Bahamas. Life has a rhythm of its own there as if the people decided to let the world rotate a bit slower. Of course, there are just as many worries, sorrows, pains and sadness as in any other part of the world. But there is more music, more love and laughter, more daydreams and dancing, more smiles and sunshine, more beauty too in the souls of those who have so little but are always willing to share. But after half a year, I had enough of it. They call it *island fever*; it makes you restless, and suddenly, that slow rhythm is not so attractive anymore. You feel like something is holding you back, that everything is happening in the world, but you're not part of it. I realized that it was time for me to leave.

I explained it to Hernando and told him that nothing would change. He would just continue operating the boat, and every three months, he would let me know the results, I would let him know where to contact me.

'I understand Bart, it often happens to people not born here, it's the island thing, mon, but mind you, once you tasted it, it's like sex. One time is never enough.' He laughed a deep belly laugh.

'You'll be back, Bart, you'll be back, and God willing, I'll be here to receive you back with wide-open arms.' There were actually tears in his eyes.

I went to the bank to say goodbye to Ronaldo and to take the balance of my account in cash.

The question now was where to go to. I had been in Indonesia, Australia, and the Bahamas and always under a burning sun. So I was going to try my luck up North for a change. But I also needed to make money. I still had a nice amount in the bank, but it didn't grow much from interest, and I did not exactly live on a low budget. I might make some money with the *Estrella del Mar* charters, but that remained to be seen over a twelve-month period. So I decided to try my luck in Alaska; I thought there must be a reason they call it *the last frontier.*

I booked a ticket to Miami and from there with Alaska Airlines a flight to Anchorage, Alaska's capital. Now, when you hear Alaska, you maybe think of Eskimos and igloos and dog sleighs and things, but no sir, not at all!" Bart made a gesture to emphasize his last statement as if to wash away from Harry's mind the arctic pictures he just painted. "It could be any city in mainland America, with high rises, overpasses and traffic jams and all.

I booked a room in the historic Anchorage Hotel in the centre of town for a week; I figured I needed some time to get my bearings. First, I opened an account with the Wells Fargo bank,

then I decided I needed transportation, so I bought a Chevy

truck with off-road tires and a winch in the front and back. It was not new but in perfect condition, and I had the feeling it would serve me well. Then I went to the humane society and found a four-year-old male Tervuren dog that jumped at me, wagging his tail like I was his long-lost master. I fell in love with it instantly. I paid for the dog and told the woman that I would come every day to see it but would come and fetch it in a week or so. I was sure the hotel would not be happy to see me walk in with a large dog the size of a timber wolf. My dog's name was Devil, and I would find out later how fitting that name was.

Across from the hotel was an eatery, where breakfasts, lunches and dinners were served and where, during weekends, live music played. It was a trendy, popular joint and I went there especially for my lunches. The owner was a burly Scottish character who sometimes played the bagpipes and was never seen without his tartan kilt. He knew his patrons and spotted a newcomer like me immediately. The first time I went there, he welcomed me, pouring a 'wee dram' for himself and for me. He lifted his glass and said '*Slàinte mhath*' – pronounced slan-ge-var – which means *good health* in Gaelic. I took a liking to him. There was a special event each Saturday night, and there wouldn't be an empty seat in the house. At precisely 7 PM, all of the guests would be waiting anxiously and hungrily at their tables. But the one and only thing on the menu that evening was haggis.

Now, mind you, haggis is not just served like any other ordinary delicacy. Haggis demands respect. It is piped in from the kitchen to the restaurant dining room with the owner wearing his Scottish regalia, marching in front and playing the bagpipes. Behind him, the chef follows, and a large serving dish is held high, with the famous haggis in the centre. Now you just don't serve a haggis, no sir; it is blessed by the owner of the place first. It starts with 'Fair fa' your honest, sonsie face, Great chieftain o the puddin'-race!', the rest I forgot. Then the owner and the chef toast each other with a whiskey, '*Slàinte mhath*', only then can the haggis be cut."

Bart was smacking his lips, like the Scottish delicacy of years gone by was still on his tongue.

"What is a haggis? Is it some kind of rare animal?" Harry wanted to know.

"No, believe it or not, it's offal."

"Offal? Like intestines and things? You're kidding me again, right?" said Harry.

"No, I'm not. It is basically sheep's pluck, minced with oatmeal, onion, suet, spices and salt, mixed with stock and cooked in a sheep's stomach. Now you may think that does not sound very appetizing, but try to explain that to a Scotsman, and you better be ready to defend yourself.

Anyway, the Scot had a daughter who helped her father with the special events' administration and organization. When it was busy, she didn't mind helping out wherever necessary; that's how I met her one day. I do not remember her as being remarkably pretty at first, but she had an extraordinary personality that served her father's business well and kept impertinent suitors at bay. Her name was Paisley, and for some unknown reason, we got along well. On a Sunday afternoon, when it was very quiet at the place, father and daughter invited me to their table. 'I don't want to be nosy, Bart', Paisley said, 'but what are your plans in Alaska? You don't strike me as the average tourist....', so I told them. I explained where I had been and what I had done, that I intended to invest some money, hoping to spend a few years there before I became restless again and move on to whatever place would take my fancy. I also told them that in the Anchorage Daily News, I read an ad offering a lumber concession for sale and that I'd thought about looking at it. 'Do you know anything about that business?' the father asked.

'Absolutely nothing,' I answered, 'but I can learn.' 'Would you like us to help you?' Paisley offered. 'Mind you, it is a very specialized business, and the players in the field are not exactly welcoming newcomers. But we know quite a few guys that may be of help to you.' 'That sounds great,' I answered, 'so what do you suggest I should do next?'

'Start by seeing Vince Taylor,' Paisley answered. 'He is a lawyer, and as honest as somebody in that profession comes, I can give him a call to introduce you. Then the next person to meet is old Brian McIver; what he doesn't know about the lumber business in Alaska is not worth knowing.' She turned to look at her father, 'That's where you come in, Dad. It may cost Bart a bottle of single malt, but it'll be worth it.'

So I made an appointment with the lawyer, but even before

that, Paisley's father called me to come over to meet Mr McIver. Old McIver, they called him. But even in his seventies, he still looked like a lumberjack with hands that could crush a coconut. He towered over most people, but in those days, I matched his length. 'So, young man,' he greeted me while putting my hand in a vice, 'you want to make your fortune in lumber, do you?' He made it sound like it was the dumbest idea he'd ever heard. Then, as if to wash the stupidity away, he emptied a tumbler of the single malt I ordered, in one swig, smacked his lips and immediately filled his glass again.

'Yes,' I answered, 'and Paisley here told me you would help me do so'.

He looked at Paisley, then at my face and laughed so loud that the bottles in the bar seemed to be shaking. 'No, seriously, sir,' I said, 'I know all too well that an expectation to make a fortune is the surest way to failure. I like to succeed with any venture I start, and I'll give it my all. But I'll never put more capital at risk than I can afford to lose.' McIver kept his gaze on me for a moment. There was a serious expression on his face when he said, 'In that case, Bart, my old friend's smart daughter was right, I can help you, with advice that is, if that is what you want.'

'Thank you,' I said, 'that is very much appreciated, but I know so little of the lumber business that I don't even know which questions to ask.'

'Did you bring that newspaper?' McIver asked. I had brought it, and I showed it to him.

'That's what I thought,' he commented after he read the ad. 'That is the Kessler concession. As it happens, he passed away, and his widow and kids are living in Europe and have no interest in the business.

Old Kessler came to Alaska shortly after the war, and the rumour went that he was an escaped Nazi. He'd built a homestead at the border of what later became his concession, but nobody wanted it in those days. It is a good concession Bart, but the Eastside is pretty well worked over. He cut good roads so access to the sawmill wouldn't be your problem, but having your lumber accepted there might be.'

'Why is that?' I asked. 'It's because the other suppliers are using virtually all the capacity the sawmill can handle, and they would gang up against you not to interfere with their business.'

'But the trees would be there?' I asked.

'Oh yes, definitely, it is a large concession, but mind you, no clear cutting, you can't touch a log less than fourteen-inch there, but there's enough of it. Do you know how much they want for it?' 'Yes, they are asking for four hundred thousand, including the cabin and some equipment.'

'Offer half, and they'll take it. Not too many will be interested in it because of the limited sawmill capacity and how the others will treat a newcomer. You must be aware of additional costs, mostly payments to the government, but Paisley can help you there. Go and see Vince Taylor; let him offer the terms to the family. If he puts the deal on paper, you can take it to the bank. Then I suggest you talk to Roy Rogers, Rogers not being his real name and not the old Western movie star, but Roy is his real name. He is the best hand you could find, and he'll run the operation like no one else I know of. Roy is from Canada, and he's never seen without his cowboy boots and hat, but he could run General Motors, I'm sure. He recently had a fall-out with the Heemstra brothers, for whom he worked more than six years. He'll be available and would work for you if I tell him you're OK.'

'Would that cost me another bottle?' I asked, pointing at the empty one on the table.

'You bet, son, you bet,' he answered, and there was that belly laugh again."

"So what happened? Did they accept your offer?" Harry wanted to know.

"Let me tell you," Bart replied.

11

"I met Roy Rogers at the end of the week. He was in his late forties and carried himself like a person who knew his business. He was six feet tall with not an inch of fat on his muscular body.

He could have been plucked from the set of Unforgiven and would have given Clint Eastwood a run for his money. Under his cowboy hat was a wild bunch of dark brown hair. His eyes were green and would look straight at you. Roy was the kind of man that put you immediately at ease. Happily, the family had accepted my offer. At first, they countered with three hundred thousand. But my lawyer proved to be worth his ten grand, as he assured them that there were no other buyers and that the one offering the two hundred thousand might walk, so they accepted. I signed the documents, paid the money and became the owner of the concession.

Attached to the documents was a map, so all that was left to do was to visit the place I'd just bought.

Roy accepted the pay I offered, he had his own truck and knew where the concession was, so I asked him to go there and wait for me at the cabin. Next thing I picked up Devil, who jumped in my truck as if to let me know, *let's go, boss, I have been in this damned place long enough.*

Then I drove over to Paisley to say goodbye, but she had different ideas".

Bart paused; he stood up from the bench to loosen his stiff muscles and straighten his body.

He put both hands against his back and bent backwards; he could not hide the fact that he was living in the autumn of his years. Still, the shadow of the sturdy adventurer he once was could not be mistaken. Stretching himself in a vain effort to regain his former length, he looked around him as the captain of a galleon searching the horizon on the open sea. He sat down again, bit on the stem of his pipe, then continued his account, pointing his pipe toward the distance as if his concession was somewhere there, hidden behind the lilac bushes.

"I have to be honest", Bart continued, "I was very curious about the property, but as is often the case with women, Paisley was more practical. 'No goodbyes yet, mister,' she said. 'You and I are going shopping first. Then I'll go with you and try to turn that old cabin into a livable place.' She was right, of course. By the time we were done shopping, my truck was loaded with groceries, tools, bedsheets and blankets, furniture, kitchen stuff, dog food and towels and all those things a guy never thinks of buying. Paisley also advised me to buy a shotgun and shells, a riffle and a revolver. It felt like she wanted me to start a revolution, but she explained there were bears, I would want to go hunting for fresh meat, and there were some aggressive rednecks in the lumber business who would never be seen without being armed. When I bought the shotgun, I asked Paisley if she expected me to murder rabbits, but of course, she did not understand.

The place I now owned was northwest of Fairbanks, a distance of about four hundred miles from Anchorage. Paisley had taken a few days off, and we left pretty early the next day, with a happy devil taking possession of the backseat of my truck. It was an eight to ten hours drive, but I wanted to arrive during daylight, so we only made one short stop for coffee and a sandwich. We left the main road at about three o'clock, finding the cabin easily after following a few old signs that read 'Kessler Property'. As we approached, we noticed a truck was parked in front, so evidently, Roy had beaten us to it.

The cabin was larger than I had expected; it had been built as a two-room log cabin first, then there had been two add-ons. There was a unit with the main room, a kitchen, and a bedroom on the right side. On the left side was a storage building. The place was properly locked, the keys came with the documents. I gave Roy the keys for the storage unit, and I opened the cabin. Everything was left as if the previous owner could come back tomorrow. Although there was a thick layer of dust on everything, and somehow packrats or squirrels had found their way inside. The furniture had holes in it, and the stuffing was all over the place. It was a mess, but the roof did not seem to be leaking, and the logs were solidly chinked. 'Darn,' Paisley quipped, 'No central vacuum cleaner and no air-conditioning either.' But I noticed that there was no water, and of course no electricity. There were several petrol lamps that would probably still work, but the water was a bigger problem. Roy came back from his inspection of the shed. 'There is an old Cat generator there and quite a bit of other equipment and tools,' he said. 'It will be dark soon, but tomorrow I'll try to get the thing started.' 'We'll have no water,' I said, 'Let me have a look,' Roy answered, and he walked around the building. When he returned, he said, 'That old Nazi wasn't stupid, there is a well outside with a sunk pump, if I get that generator running tomorrow, we'll have water and light, boss.'

The three of us emptied the cabin, piling everything for now up behind the building. Then with the brooms and brushes we bought, we cleaned the place as best as we could, opening doors and windows to let the stale air out. We threw the mattresses out, but the beds were solid forged iron, so I decided to keep them. I told Roy that he could take the guest cabin, there was no mattress, but he'd brought a sleeping bag, so that was OK. We would buy some other stuff later in Fairbanks."

Harry had absorbed every word, waiting for a question that he would have liked to ask much earlier, "Did you sleep with her?"

Bart guffawed, "You old goat, what business is that of yours? But if it makes you happy, yes I did, but not right then, much later. And this is why.

When we bought furniture in Anchorage, Paisley picked a couch and two fauteuils. I'd said, 'What the hell is that for?' but she insisted. 'Wait, sailor', she called me sailor after I told her my story, 'there will be very cold evenings and very lonely nights. You'll be happy to have something comfortable in your cabin when the blizzard howls around it.'

There was only one bedroom in the main cabin with one double bed. Paisley addressed the elephant in the room with her usual vigour. 'Listen, sailor, I am not going to sleep with you, not that you would steal my virginity, it's too late for that, but I know that you are in transfer here, and I'm not going to break my heart again.' *She said again, so there must be a heartache there, but now is not the time to ask questions about it,* I thought.

'I understand and appreciate that, Paisley,' I said, 'and no problem, I'll be happy to sleep on the couch. I'll use a blanket to fight the cold and my imagination to fight temptation.' Paisley laughed.

Now let me teach you something about women, Harry. She may tell you that she wont sleep with you, and you accept that, but don't ever make the mistake of letting her know that's quite alright with you. She'll have your balls for breakfast. Not a single woman in the world takes it as a compliment not to be desired."

Harry looked at Bart's face in wonder. What the hell did that sailor think he would do with that advice about women? It came some fifty years too late. Besides, he understood more about Pelargonium Peltatum than he ever did about women.

"Anyway, we were all tired, so we turned in early. Devil

instinctively understood what was expected of him, and he laid down beside the couch, ready to defend his benefactor.

The next morning, I woke up from his growling; Paisley came out of the bedroom in a bathrobe, 'Time for breakfast, sailor', she said, which meant that I had to get up to make a fire in the stove. Luckily there were still tinder-dry logs stacked next to it, so within minutes, she was frying eggs and bacon while I made coffee. Suddenly several lights started to come on, and rusty water spurted from the tap, followed by a steady flow of clear water. Roy came in smiling, 'Morning boss, mam, that was easy, those old Cats seldom let you down, enough diesel fuel for quite a while in there.'

After breakfast, practical Paisley started to write down what we still needed. Unfortunately, the freezer and fridge were badly ridden with mould, so we threw those out. We also required furniture for Roy, a short-wave radio set, walkie-talkies, and several new heavy chainsaws. However, there were some in the shed we could still use, so Paisley asked Roy to check the shed and give her a list of things that he still needed to be purchased. I decided that she and Roy would go together to Fairbanks to see if they could find it all there, I gave her the money I thought she might need, and they left. Then, for the first time, I was alone in the cabin where I thought I might spend several years of my life.

This was as good a time as any to see what my dog could do, so to make sure he couldn't run away from me chasing some animal tracks, I put him on a long line. He just sat at my knee when I did and looked at me like he was saying, *no need, boss,*

I'm well trained and, as it turned out, he was. So we walked around the premises; the previous owner had cleared quite an area surrounding the place, mainly for security. As a result, no grizzly or other danger could approach unseen. I soon realized Devil was very well trained, so I unleashed him. 'Kneel', I ordered, and he immediately sat down beside my leg. 'Down', I said, and he obeyed. 'Stay', I said, and I walked away some thirty paces, but he didn't move. I whistled once, and he ran to me to sit at my knee again. I knew that Tervurens, a longhaired Belgian shepherd breed with a totally black face, were very intelligent dogs, often used by the police and army. This one must have been a working dog, and I had been lucky to find him. There was one more thing to try out, but that could be done later.

I could not do much more than checking the shed, and to my surprise, there was quite a bit of equipment, tools, parts and everything nicely organized. One thing about Germans is that their Punktlichkeit (punctuality) always shows. The generator was mounted on a concrete footing and rubber buffers; that's why we did not hear the noise in the cabin."

"Was there a garden around the house?" Harry asked.

"A garden?" Bart laughed, "no way, man, nobody has time to water the daisies there, and don't think of a cabin in the forest as a house in Amsterdam. What we call a blokhut, a log cabin, is built out of trees that are usually cut right there, where a cabin is wanted. The logs are sort of piled one on top of the other; only the corners were cut square so they would fit. The walls are the same inside and outside, just clean trees without the bark, and the space between the logs is filled-in with dried moss, they call that chinking, so if you build one, you save a lot of money on wallpaper. The windows are small, and you need wooden shutters and a strong door because bears are smart and can get in when you're not there; they make a hell of a mess. No, my friend, there would not be a great demand for your profession there."

Harry had forgotten all about the garden already. He imagined finding a grizzly in his kitchen, which gave him the creeps. The only wildlife invasion in his workman's cottage he could think of was a fieldmouse, but he realized that a bear raiding your fridge could be worse than a teenage son.

"So, when Paisley and Roy returned with another truckload", Bart continued, "I thought *if this continues, all my money will be gone before we cut a single tree.* But when I saw what they'd purchased, I had to agree with everything. We installed the fridge and the freezer, and that night we had a barbeque and some cold beer. The following day Roy and I were going to scout the concession to make a plan of action. I found out that Roy was a man of many talents.

There was a sturdy off-road vehicle with heavy swamp tires, a bit beaten up, but Roy got it running in fifteen minutes. Paisley wanted to organize the cabin further, so Roy and I left, taking the rifle and some sandwiches and water with us. Paisley kept the revolver. She claimed she could outshoot Annie Oakley, so we shouldn't worry about her.

The main road cuts through the concession from a fishbone pattern of paths that reached further into the forest. The first hour we were riding through a rather dense section, but Roy pointed out that most trees were young and the biggest ones less than ten inches thick. That was the part the German had worked over. Some two hours later, after stopping once for a grizzly on our path and a couple of times for a crossing moose, we reached the part that wasn't touched. Now I noticed the difference: giant trees with trunks as thick as a truck tire reached for the sky among the smaller growth. 'Here it is, boss', Roy said, 'we got to cut our way into it, but plenty of good lumber here'. I could see that, but how the hell were we going to get that to the one and only sawmill, miles away from our property?

'Leave that to me, boss', Roy assured me, 'We do the cutting, and Wilder will do the transportation. I know him as a friend, and he'll take our business, nobody to intimidate Peter Wilder. The sawmill might be another problem, though.'

'Shouldn't we make sure that the mill is willing to take our lumber before we start cutting?' I wondered. 'Yes, boss, I'm afraid we have no other choice.'

'Well, we'll see about that, but no more *yes boss no boss*, please Roy, we'll work together for a long time, I hope. So just call me Bart.' 'Well, I beg your pardon, sir, but I won't feel comfortable with that; I'm a bit old fashioned, you know. We'll have lumberjacks working for us soon – not good if they'll see me being too familiar, boss.' I saw his point, so I agreed, but later we became great friends, and that boss thing disappeared automatically. We made our way through the thick underbrush to inventory the number of harvestable trees, but Roy's experienced eyes soon had seen enough, 'This could be great, boss, if we can process it, you may be in the money.'

It was late afternoon when we were back at the cabin, and it was a completely different place. There was a fire burning in the fireplace; delicious smells wafted from the kitchen, and on the table was an artistic arrangement of various twigs. A smiling Paisley asked, 'How was it? Oh, and this is happy hour, so what would you gentlemen like to drink?' I thought, if this is life in the forest, I may have found Nirvana, but it was going to be quite different.

'Do you know the owners of the sawmill?' I asked Roy when we were sitting down drinking a beer. 'Sure, but he is a strange bird, his father built the sawmill, and he took over after the old man died. Whatever he did with the money he made, he sure didn't invest it in the sawmill. It is old, and the capacity is limited. That's why the other guys won't be happy to see somebody restarting the Kessler operation. And to be honest, they won't be happy knowing I'm involved.'

'Well, let's go see him tomorrow,' I decided, knowing very well that without the ability to process my lumber, the value of the concession was zero.

12

The owner of the sawmill was a packrat. The sawmill resembled a junkyard more than the processing plant handling the supply of several lumber operations in the area. Discarded pieces of engines, empty barrels, worn tires, car wrecks, and other rubbish that must have been collected over the years were strewn all over the property. It did not require much expertise to realize that improving the ill-maintained plant wouldn't take much.

The owner was a slovenly dressed, uninterested character who hesitated at first to even talk to me. Still, he seemed to be impressed enough by Roy's reputation that he was willing to listen.

The yard had two operational lines; a third was discarded due to the need for a new Caterpillar and several parts. There was not much cut material ready for transportation piled on the yard, despite the significant demand for Alaskan white wood. But there were enormous piles of cut-offs, odd pieces and discarded material from processing the many thousands of logs over the years. It took quite a while for the owner to be comfortable talking to us, but slowly he loosened up. He confessed that for the past number of years, he had wanted to quit and go back to his hometown of Columbia, South Carolina, and retire, but there had been no takers for the yard. The way it looked, I was not surprised.

'How much would you want for it?' I asked impulsively, not thinking for a moment to become the owner. 'Half a million,' he answered. I looked at Roy, who furtively nodded. 'That seems a bit stiff,' I replied, bluffing, of course having no clue. 'Let me get back to you tomorrow, but not a word to anybody or I won't even think about a counter-offer.'

When we drove back, Roy said, 'I believe I see your line of thinking, boss: if we own the mill, we kill two birds with one stone, our lumber will be cut, and those other guys can swallow their objections or build their own sawmill, which I am sure they won't.'

We were in for a horrible surprise when we reached the cabin. Paisley was in tears. She told us that three ruffians had come to look for the new owner and give him a message: *Better go back where you came from, we don't need you here.* She told them it was none of their business and that I now owned the concession. They then made a terrible mess of the interior, and one of them, a short sort of a guy with one white eye like that of a putrefied fish and the smell of it as well, hit Paisley in the face. The side of which was bruised.

I was livid.

'Shorty Fowler,' Roy said, 'the goddamn coward. A piece of shit – sorry, mam – that works for the Heemstra brothers. You want me to take care of him, boss?'

But I realized I needed to keep my cool, it was only the two of us, and I was sure we would face a whole gang. 'No, Roy,' I said, 'as much as I would like to kill the coward myself, there are better ways for revenge. So you stay here with Paisley; I'll go back to Anchorage tomorrow morning and be back in a few days. That ok with you, Paisley?' She said it was but begged me not to tell her father or he would send in the army.

When I arrived in Anchorage, I went straight to my lawyer and told him the essentials of a business plan I thought of while driving. He wrote it down and translated it in the wording bankers understand. Without issues, the bank was willing to extend a line of credit of four hundred thousand dollars against my signature and the concession as security; of course, they knew I was still good for the money. I then went to Paisley's dad and lied that everything was fine, and she was happy doing what she was doing but would soon come back home.

Back at the cabin, it was like nothing ever happened there, Paisley was her happy self, and the place felt welcoming again. I explained what I had been doing in town, and both Roy and Paisley thought it was an excellent idea. Then the next day, I sent Roy to Fairbanks, where he was able to drum up a dozen of the best lumberjacks he knew who'd worked for him before.

He did not disappoint me. A few days later, a bunch of guys showed up that resembled an Olympic rugby team, with a giant from Barbados as foreman.

In the meantime, Paisley and I went to the sawmill and sat

down with the owner, who seemed to have taken his weekly shower, making himself somewhat more presentable for the occasion.

We shook hands on a purchase price of five hundred thousand, of which three hundred thousand down, and the balance payable in two instalments of a hundred thousand each year following the date of transfer of ownership. It meant we had to go down to Anchorage again. My dog protested loudly, but when I said 'stay', he seemed to understand. In the city, we first met with my lawyer, then with the bank manager. We signed the documents, the three hundred thousand was transferred, and I was the owner of the sawmill. The lawyer proposed to put the mill in a separate company, which we did. I called it BARLEY SAWMILLS LTD., which was, of course, a combination of my name and Paisley's, but what's in a name? And anyway, she was delighted.

She told her dad she wanted to stay another two weeks. He objected at first but gave in when she explained why and what the arrangements in the cabin were like. If an extra hand was needed, he could always find temporary help, especially for his haggis evenings.

Before we went back, an artist made a big sign for me, BARLEY SAWMILLS LTD., and we bought a few bottles of champagne.

What a team of hard-working men are able to accomplish in a few days was apparent when we returned. Beside the path, a few hundred yards before reaching our cabin, was a fresh clearing, and on it, an elongated building of roughly sawn timber that was going to sleep our workers was nearly finished. The building was divided into sixteen small cabins, no luxury, but a good place to sleep for tired lumberjacks. With Roy very much in charge, they were erecting another building where they could cook and eat; one of the men we hired was the camp cook. Roy and the cook went to Fairbanks and came back with a stove, a large freezer and fridge, and all those things a camp cook needs. The shop had no problem extending credit, but I sent the money the next day and opened an account for the chef.

Three more days and the workers camp was completed. The men claimed to be used to sleeping in hammocks or on pallets in sleeping bags, but I ordered them to make proper bunk beds, and I bought the mattresses, pillows and blankets.

After that, it was time for a celebration."

In the park in Amsterdam, an old man with a dark complexion and a white beard, pushing what resembled an oil barrel with wheels, a rake, and broom clipped to either side, shuffled to the trash bin in front of the two old men. He was wearing a long grey tunic of some sort under a worn-out jacket and a round knitted white headgear. He was busy emptying the trash when two young brats on bicycles passed, shouting at the old man standing in their way, 'Watch it, Mohamed, you're not in Morocco.'

"I would love to get my hands on those snotnoses," Harry fulminated, "no respect for an old man trying to make a living cleaning up the garbage they leave. Don't you think he would rather be in his country if he could provide for his family there?"

"I guess so", Bart responded non-committedly, "it's just these religious Muslim fanatics that give their own people a bad rap. I think that everybody should be free to believe in whatever he wants to believe in. As a young boy, I was catholic because my parents were. Although, later, as a sailor, I found God in the infinity of the oceans. What I don't like is the arrogance of them calling us infidels. I respect their religion but don't call me a heathen because my God has a different name."

"I agree," said Harry, "I am always willing to give anybody the same respect I receive from them, but there was no reason for those scoundrels to insult that old man just because he is a Muslim."

Ignorant of the discussion about him, the old man nodded and beamed a friendly smile at the two seniors on the bench enjoying a sunny afternoon. Then, slightly stooped, he shuffled along, pushing his cart to the next bin.

"Wanna hear the rest of my story?" Bart asked, knowing the answer. Harry just nodded.

"As I said, it was time for a celebration. So we all went to the sawmill, Roy with all the men he hired. The first thing we did was nail the sign with the new name on two posts at the yard entrance. Roy had talked to the previous owner's men and fired three of them right away, but four seemed to be good hands, and Roy advised to keep those.

Then we opened the champagne and all toasted to the future of our undertaking. It was the first time Paisley kissed me, only on my cheek, mind, but it felt as if something permanent was implanted there. Now, being the owner of a concession and a sawmill was nice. Still, thus far, I had done many things that only cost me money, and I was eager to start what I was supposed to do: cut and sell trees. Nevertheless, it was practical Paisley who convinced me to first clean up the yard, using all the hands on our payroll, then while making the third line operational again, start cutting trees and have Peter Wilder bring in the first truck loads. And that's precisely what we did, and when we were done, it looked like an entirely different, very professional operation. The four hands we kept were delighted with the changes and worked like horses, and with the help of two of Roy's men, they got all three lines running full speed.

Of course, what happened next was exactly what we expected and what we were prepared for.

The Heemstra brothers showed up at the mill with half a dozen goons who were supposed to intimidate us. They walked straight to the shed that functioned as the yard's office, where Roy and I were waiting for them.

'You that guy who bought Kessler's place?' one of them, seemingly a Heemstra who'd forgotten to introduce himself, asked. He was a burly character, carrying a large revolver very visibly on his hip. 'We don't need you here, mister. This here sawmill's capacity is fully booked, no room for strangers son, beat it'.

Now, this Heemstra guy was just a stupid dumbass who would have seen the sign at the entrance and the three lines running in a cleaned-up yard. I would deal with him, but one of the cowboys in his posse was a short guy with a white eye like that of a dead fish. I tightened my fists, and I noticed Roy becoming restless. 'Who are you?' I addressed the man who just spoke. He did not seem to expect that question. 'Who I am, you'll find out, what I want, I told you, mister. So don't you smartass me.' I smiled at him. 'Listen, Lucky Luke,' I said, through my teeth, 'why don't you look behind you? I don't remember having invited you to my sawmill, and for your information, no loads from the Heemstra brothers will be processed here.' He looked as if a rattler just bit him. Still, when he glanced over his shoulder, he saw half a dozen of my men behind the Bahamian foreman, all pointing shotguns at his posse. Then from behind my office, another half dozen men, also pointing shotguns appeared. The asshole got the message.

'You the owner of the sawmill?' he asked, sounding perplexed.

'Now you seem to be less stupid than you look,' I answered. He didn't seem to know what to do next. Finally, the foolish goon turned around and indicated to his men that they would leave.

'One moment, bozo,' I said in a friendly way, 'you are free to leave after you put all your weapons down right where you are standing, except for that little piece of shit there who apparently likes fighting so much that he hits women.' The coward looked at his boss with terror in his eyes, pleading for protection. But the boss put his revolver on the ground, and all his men did the same. 'Let's go,' he said. 'Not you,' to shorty, who started to wet himself, afraid that he was going to be killed."

"Did you kill him?" Harry seemed to hope for an affirmative

answer. "What an asshole to knock a woman down when you are with a bunch of guys, and she can't defend herself."

"No, course not. Murder is murder, but we locked him up for two days and nights. When we eventually unlocked the door, he cried like a baby, and he had defecated on himself. Roy gave him a kick in his shitty pants and said, 'Get the hell out of here, you skunk. Don't ever let me see you in Alaska again, or by God, I'll wring your stinking neck'. To this day, I have never seen a guy run faster, and we never saw him again.

From there on, things went as smooth as can be. The Heemstra brothers came back, but this time without guns or posse. Instead, they were there with cap in hand. Shorty had been fired, and they asked what they could do to make it up to the lady.' Get her a nice young horse', I said because I knew she loved to ride. So they did, and Paisley fell in love with it. Roy built her a stable. But now Paisley went back to help her father and only came for the weekends, although I could tell her heart was here.

I missed her. Her female presence enhanced life in the forest, and she became such a good friend; all the guys loved and respected her.

With all three lanes running at full capacity and able to handle the supply of all producers, I was soon able to repay the bank and also the remaining balance I owed the previous owner. The demand for our product seemed unsatisfiable. But not only did my bank account grow so also did the already large pile of cut-offs and sawdust. It was Roy who came with the brilliant idea to build a huge drying kiln, so we could sell kiln-dried lumber, which made a better price and at the same time got rid of the waste. We built it ourselves, and it was not only huge; it was revolutionary as well. We built a large furnace at some fifty yards distance from the kiln to avoid the risk of accidental fire. A duct that could be regulated forced the heat into the kiln, which had openings on all four sides to expel the moisture. There were separate roads to both, to load and unload lumber to the kiln and one to feed the furnace. I had to buy additional equipment, but I had the budget for it; we made even more money after the kiln became operational. Loading, drying, and unloading took twenty-four hours, and the kiln had overcapacity. That is, we could not saw what the kiln could handle. So we decided to build a fourth line, with the latest equipment available. We also extended the workers camp and hired ten additional hands. Peter Wilder purchased two extra flat-bed trucks to haul the large number of trees we were now cutting. The Alaska forest management policy ensures that young trees are getting a chance to flourish, and as a result, reforestation is a natural process.

Paisley took care of my finances. Following her advice, I hired a woman as the bookkeeper at the mill, and she soon cracked the whip there. For the first time, the administration was well organized. Paisley told me that I was a millionaire, not counting the market value of the smooth-running operation of BARLEY SAWMILLS LTD., and the large concession accessible through the road system we built. Roy turned out to be a gifted manager indeed, but as a result, there was very little need for my involvement. I went to Anchorage more often to see my lawyer and the bank, but I realized that I actually went to see Paisley. That's when we became lovers. I will spare you the details, but I made no promises, and Paisley understood and respected that.

I sometimes went hunting to have fresh meat for the camp and ourselves. Roy turned out to be a capable chef, and we ate well. One day I was not far into the woods, looking for grouse, when I was suddenly confronted by a giant black bear who reared not twenty yards in front of me. My shotgun was loaded with birdshot pellets which would kill a grouse but do absolutely nothing to a bear. This all happened in a split second, and I feared for my life. Suddenly Devil jumped from behind me, and in one great leap, he was on the bear. Now, even a big dog is no match for a bear, but Devil was as quick as a cat. Every time the bear tried to hit him with his sharp claw, Devil jumped just beyond his reach, then, with the speed of light, he bit the bear somewhere. I feared for the life of my dog, but the bear had no interest in me anymore. Soon the bear became bored and just slowly retreated among the brush. Devil came heavily panting to my knee, wagging his tail, and sat down as if to say, *danger gone, boss*. I noticed blood seeping from his side, where the bear must have almost fatally hit him. I had nothing to dress the wound, so I took off my shirt, and after winding it around his body, the bleeding stopped. I took him to a vet in Fairbanks who stitched the wound.

I had been in Alaska for almost three years now, spending most of the time in the bush or in my cabin. I was getting restless again, wondering how the rest of the world was doing. Paisley was the first one to notice it. 'The sea calling again, sailor?' she said one evening when we were in bed in my cabin. 'I am going to miss you, Bart, but you'll always be in my heart.'

I felt sort of bad about it, but I knew my time in Alaska was over."

"But why?" Harry asked, not understanding why Bart would want to leave when he'd made so much money.

"That's not an easy question to answer," Bart paused as if to find the right formulation for what was to follow. "You know Harry," he continued, "money is nice to have, I have been poor, and I have been rich and poor again. Believe me, I know. Now don't misunderstand me; life is much easier if you've got it. People treat you different, with respect even, which is silly because you can be very rich and very stupid at the same time. Don't you believe those smart-asses telling you that money can't make you happy – that's nice to know if you never had it. But does that imply that happiness is the prerogative of the poor? Nonsense, my friend. Though making money should never be a goal in itself and having money, being rich, I mean, is only meaningful if you do the right thing with it. If money can't buy you happiness, it can't buy you a place in heaven either. For me, there was not a fortune big enough to keep me somewhere where I didn't want to be. I was born with a wandering soul, and nothing was going to change that.

So I asked Paisley to supervise the sale of my property in

cooperation with the lawyer and the bank while I was gone. When all was complete, there was a balance of five million, four hundred and fifty thousand dollars in my account in Anchorage alone. In addition, there was still a positive balance in Australia and an accrued amount in the Bahamas from the fishing boat. So now I found myself in Florida, enjoying the sun after three years in Alaska, putting up with some harsh winters.

It pained me to have left Paisley behind and also my fantastic dog, but travelling with a huge dog was virtually impossible, so I gave him to Roy, who was on cloud nine with him.

I sent instructions to my bank to pay a very generous bonus to Roy and a nice one to each of my workers. I bought a cottage with stables and a large pasture for Paisley and gifted the funds to purchase several horses of her choice. I left letters of recommendation about Roy and my employees for the new owners, who indeed continued their employment."

"So, where did you go next?" Harry was curious, hoping this was not the end of the adventures.

"Africa," answered Bart, "I'd always wanted to see Africa."

13

While in Florida, I met this historian, who was born in Monrovia, the capital of Liberia in West Africa. He was a sympathetic sort of a man, about my age, an associate professor at Harvard University. He was on vacation. I planned to go fishing and see Hernando and Ronaldo, so I invited him to come along. We chartered a plane to take us there, and he insisted on paying half, which I accepted only to make him feel better.

Hernando received me with an enormous bear hug, and I introduced Vincent to him, 'Welcome, sir,' he said. 'A friend of Bart's is a friend of mine.' Hernando took us out, and we had a great day. You know already that I'm always happy being at sea, but when you're out fishing, you want to catch something. Half an hour out, Johny shouted 'FISH ON', 'Go ahead,' I told Vincent, and he landed the first Dorado, 'Man, that was fun,' he said with a big smile after I poured the traditional cold beer over his head. We landed six more, and I hooked a massive barracuda. It was a great day out, and I learned enough about Liberia to decide to make that my next destination.

That night we dined with Ronaldo, who was also happy to

see me. He told me about his promotion, and the asshole who used to be his superior was no longer at the bank. There was an amount of one hundred and ten thousand in the *Estrella del Mar* joint account.

I told Ronaldo to transfer it to Hernando's account and close the one we held jointly. Then, when we left the next day, I handed a very emotional Hernando the papers of our boat; it was now his.

The next day we flew back, and I booked a ticket to Monrovia. I said goodbye to Vincent, who thanked me profusely, gave me a few necessary contact addresses and suggested we should stay in touch. I forgot to mention because I didn't consider it important, that Vincent was black. I am absolutely colourblind and convinced that all people are created equal, and unlike many adhering to the American Declaration of Independence, I do practice what I believe in. I am telling you that because it is important for the rest of my story.

After the abolition in America, that is when slavery was finally abolished, there were a bunch of well-meaning Americans who thought it should be possible for emancipated slaves to go back to Africa if they wanted. They established the A.C.S., (American Colonization Society). They bought a ship and sponsored the settlement of an initial few thousand freed slaves; I believe it was in 1820 or so, then later they also sent ex-slaves from the Caribbean. Now, don't think that was altruism. They just wanted to get rid of them after they were 'free'. But of course, there were already people living in what is now Liberia. That was no problem for the so-called Americo Liberians, who were bigger than the local population and considered the locals primitives, so they enslaved the latter. For many years the shots in Liberia were called by the newcomers. When I decided to go there, a political group of about one hundred fifty thousand Americo Liberians controlled the country of more than a million inhabitants. The man in power was President Tubman, the Liberian flag resembled the American flag, same stripes but one star only, the capital was named after James Monroe, an American President, and American dollars are in use as the local currency. A strange story Vincent told me, but him being a professor, I believed it, and because I was curious about Africa, I thought it was not a bad place to start.

I booked a house at the Riverside Villa Hotel, which would give me the privacy I wanted with domestic help at the same time. Vince had given me several addresses and notes for the owners, as I told you already. I first went to a car dealer, who received me with a big smile and the typical Liberian handshake, which includes snapping each other's third finger after the shake; it needs a bit of practice. He had a fully decked Landrover that I liked, complete with air conditioning, an extra fuel tank, a water tank, a secret compartment like a strongbox for valuables, gun holders, and the windows, and both sides were bulletproof. It was the kind of unit the police or the military would order, but the dealer ordered two on spec. It was perfectly legal to own one. I asked him to paint the car in jungle camouflage, build in a VHF radio communication system with an extended antenna, if he could arrange the licence.

He said he could. I had sent half a million dollars to the I.B. Bank in Monrovia, a bank with a solid reputation. The car would be ready in two days. I also received a letter of introduction to the chief of police, and that was my next visit.

The head of police was quite willing to see me when I told him who sent me.

'How is my old friend doing in America? Is he making those youngsters there finally a bit smarter?' he quipped. 'Sit down, please sit down, Mr, eh….' 'Bouman, Bart Bouman, Sir,' I quickly introduced myself. The police chief was a tall, muscular man, obviously an Americo Liberian, but I was told a foreigner should never mention that. However, he was a friendly man, and after reading Vince's letter, he nodded slowly, sat back in his chair and putting the letter down, he said, 'Regrettably true, Mr Bouman.' 'Bart, please, sir,' I said. 'Well, regrettably true, Bart. There is crime in every country, but the budgets to fight it are quite different. Liberia is not all over a safe place, and I am afraid it's especially not for white newcomers. I am ashamed to have to say that, but again regrettably, it is true. My great friend Vince, a man I greatly respect, speaks highly about you and advises me to accept you as a friend, so with your consent Bart, I am offering my friendship'. He extended his hand, which I enthusiastically shook. 'In private, it's Joseph, Bart. Chief will do when my men are present,' my new friend commented. 'What Vince is asking in his letter is to help you to find the most capable man, bodyguard and driver, to be with you all the time, and I just happen to know a man like that. His name is Lionel. He is an ethnic Liberian, a Bassa. He went to the Methodist Episcopal University, then to the army, where he became a sniper and a weapon expert. He is a Sambo instructor for which he went to Russia and a Krav Maga fighter which he learned in Israel. He was the personal bodyguard for the American ambassador until he was called back to America. Lionel is employed by the police now, but to be honest, I don't have a real job for him, and his salary compared to being a personal bodyguard is very low, but all I can offer him.'

I met Lionel the next morning. He was maybe 5'3" but as solidly built as a bull. Although I was a head taller and in great shape, I would hate to have to wrestle with him. His dark sparkling eyes looked straight at me from an intelligent face with a serious expression that easily morphed into happy laughter. I liked him.

'Lionel,' I said, 'I am going to offer you employment. The chief recommended you highly; however, I don't have a clue yet what the job is actually going to be.

I just arrived in your country and still have to decide if, and what to undertake here, so for now, you'll be my driver, bodyguard, guide and advisor and maybe translator if that's necessary.'

'I can knit socks and do laundry too, Bwana,' he said.

I looked at him perplexed, noticed the twinkle in his eyes, and we both laughed till our eyes teared up. *Intelligent humour, too*, I thought, *great!*

'I understand, sir', he quickly added, 'and I am a very flexible person.'

'I have no clue what salaries are like here, Lionel,' I said, 'but I will pay you whatever you're worth to me. I'll start with four thousand dollars per month.'

Lionel said nothing for a few moments, 'That'll be more than five times what I'm making now, sir, to be honest, so I would be delighted to accept your offer.'

'Great, then consider yourself hired. The first thing we'll do is this: I purchased a specially-equipped Landrover that we're taking delivery of in two days. So let's go there right now and tell me what you think of it.'

When Lionel saw the car, he smiled. 'The chief would give his right arm for that thing, sir, but he'll never have that much room in his budget.' 'Is that so?' I said. Then, looking at the second unit, 'How would that one look different from the one I bought if it were a police vehicle?' I asked. 'Just like the other one, sir, those are the police colours. It would need the lights and siren, of course, and the police radio. Other than that, it would be a perfect strike unit to send a special force unit out for quick action. As for the one you bought, I can think of only one thing to add, sir, a steel cable winch in the front and the back.'

Two days later, we went to pick up both units, and the dealer was very pleased I took both cars off his hands. Lionel drove ours; I took the other one. We went to the police head office where the chief was surprised to see us. 'You have a second, Chief?' I asked. 'I would like to show you something.' There was a big question on Joseph's face, but he stepped out of his office. He looked at the two units we'd parked in front; there was envy in his eyes. Without explanation, I handed him the keys to the second car.

'What's that supposed to mean?' he asked, understandably.

'Chief,' I said, 'Vincent explained to me how challenging your task here is, how dedicated you are to your country, your city and the people. Lionel pointed out how useful a car like this would be for your force. Well, sir, please accept this as a gift without any strings attached; may it make your work just a fraction easier.' The chief was speechless, 'Well, I'll be damned! I am not going to refuse, Bart! There are no pending issues between my office and you that might have been reason to reject your generosity. This indeed is a tremendous addition to our force, and I thank you from the bottom of my heart,' he gushed as he pumped my hand. 'Vincent wrote to me already informing me that you are a wealthy and generous entrepreneur. Keep that between us. Lionel will have your back at all times, and he is the best, but be careful, my friend, be very careful.'

It had just been an impulsive thing to do, but I realized that I'd made a real friend, and as it happens, it would turn out to be very important.

The next day we walked around the city, just to get an impression. It was a typical African, chaotic, disorderly and noisy city. There were colourfully dressed women peddling merchandise they carried on their head, a baby tied to their back, and young boys kicking a soccer ball or hawking a collection of bras shaped and in the pattern and colour of beach balls. It was humid and hot, and there was trash all over, although several city employees were sweeping the streets. But there was also laughter and music, and I noticed what I had seen in other countries, that poverty and exuberance is not a contradiction. On both sides of the centre street were shops, most of them owned by Lebanese merchants. If there were a million people in Liberia, they seemed to all be present at that very moment doing something in the centre street of Monrovia. But there were also office and government buildings, embassies and expensive houses, men and women fashionably dressed busying along and shiny black cars fighting their way through the melee. I did not feel unsafe. Of course, I had Lionel with me, but I doubt if it would have been different without him, though that may have been my ignorance at the time. Policemen were patrolling in twos in the busy centre street. They greeted Lionel jovially, snapping a handshake, and lanky youngsters abruptly turned their faces away when they spotted him.

We sat down in the comfort of an air-conditioned restaurant, surprisingly Swiss, and we ate a tasty meal and drank a cold beer.

'So Lionel, tell me about Liberia. Not its history, I read up on that, but what is the country like today?' Lionel thought for a moment but seemed to expect the question.

'As you must have seen, sir, Monrovia is basically a harbour city. It is a freeport significantly expanded during the Second World War by American forces. Therefore, although we have the capacity, our export is regrettably limited to a few commodities, like latex and iron ore.

We used to export palm oil and hardwood as well, but both have disappeared from the market for some reason. There is a limited production of cement, tiles, bricks, furniture, building materials and clothing. Still, it is all mainly for the local market, and we are less than two million people. Our standard of living is rather low; many live on a few dollars a day, unemployment is high, and criminality is rife as a result of it. But it is not all doom and gloom, sir. Africa is awakening. The desire to do our own thing is palpable and not just in politics. Potentially we are a rich country, but it will take time and suffering to get there. Sorry, sir, I may be getting ahead of myself.'

'Not at all, Lionel, this is of great help; Obviously, I did not come to your country as a tourist or to dwell on centre street. Why don't we make a list of whatever we would need to tour the country, then let's do some shopping? What about guns? Can you take care of that?'.

'No problem, sir, I've got all we need, including the licences.'

When we wrote down what we thought to be needed, it was a long list. The Landrover was equipped with a luggage rack, and we tied duffel bags with tents and camping equipment on it, as well as six Jerrycans with fuel. Provisions were put inside. The Liberian store owners were very pleased with our arrival, and they all threw in something extra, 'Our prices are the best, sir, come back to Hassan, sir,' they pleaded. Lionel drove me to the bank, 'Sir, please take one dollar and five-dollar notes; you are going to need it, no need to show bigger notes.' So I did, but also with an additional ten thousand dollars that I locked away in the secret safe box of the car.

It was mid-September, close to the end of the rainy season. However, we could still expect occasional tropical downpours and virtually impassable roads.

We left early the next morning, heading for Buchanan. From there, we would travel to Greenville, Barclayville, then to Zwedru and Nimba, where I wanted to see the iron ore mining project. It would take us along the west coast first, then close to the Ivory Coast in the south, along the Guinea border northeast, then close to Sierra Leone in the North. Finally, heading back to Monrovia after visiting the Firestone rubber plantation in Harbel, we would have circled the entire country.

I was curious to see the rest of the country after having seen Monrovia. Driving through Buchanan, after crossing a river with a dilapidated ferry, I wondered if my Landrover would make it across, but we did. A group of locals, women in colourful wraps, men in shorts only, and a single man in a pair of trousers, occupied the narrow spaces around our car, loudly gesticulating and arguing. Most of them were on bare feet, two men in rubber boots, a few were wearing T-shirts with political slogans.

The men kept an envious gaze on the functional vehicle and its attractive contents but spotted the police lights and logo. I started to understand the police chief's warning. Quite a few men carried a machete which I soon learned was one of their main tools, and a weapon they always kept sharp. To call Buchanan a city was being very generous, maybe fifteen or twenty thousand people, I thought. It had general stores, many small local ones and some large warehouses close to shore.

The city consisted of a collection of different houses, many self-constructed. Some, the villas of the city, were built with cement blocks and planks, including a second floor and corrugated sheets instead of a thatched roof. There were no paved roads, and the houses were randomly situated. Some buildings were entirely built from concrete blocks with white, yellow or pink painted plaster facades. A place with a torn Liberian flag flying from the roof housed the seat of the local authorities. The police, the jail, the customs, the tax collector, the hospital, the department of education, and a hotel, all under one roof. As in so many smaller countries with a limited population, the capital was a completely different world than the townships, hamlets, and little villages in the country's interior. I decided to walk. There was a sort of a market going that day; at the end of the main street was a wooden church and the closest thing to a taverna with a few rooms. We parked in front of it. 'This is why you need the small-dollar bills, sir,' Lionel said.

Buchanan was not really a tourist destination, so the market was not large. It was more a number of improvised stalls with fruit, vegetables, rice, some bush meat, eggs and live chickens, lemonades and miscellaneous canned goods, clothing and general merchandise. At several tables on plastic chairs, people ate from large plastic plates, enormous portions of palm nuts, and cooked chicken with a lot of hot peppers and rice. There was a small stand with an elderly couple sitting on an old blanket with a collection of woodcarvings on the ground around them. It immediately caught my eye; they were of an extraordinary quality, carved from a dark brownish hardwood. Several of the statues seemed to represent twins, holding on to each other. It was stylised, beautified reality, pure art. 'Fertility dolls,' Lionel explained. 'These are Fante people from Takoradi.' 'Can you ask them how much those are?' I said, pointing at two pieces I particularly liked. For twenty dollars, they were both mine. I felt guilty almost stealing those incredible pieces for so little money, but then value is a relative thing. 'They are very happy, sir. They thank you and are praying that your wife will soon bear a child,' Lionel laughed, 'they will have money to eat this week.'

After a drink at one of the two tables in front of the taverna, we continued our trip to Greenville, some 150 miles from Monrovia.

Outside Buchanan on the side of the sandy road with dense forest on one side and the sea close on the other, barefoot women walked carrying white enamel bowls on their heads. They were loaded with various things like enormous fish, coconuts, or a bunch of bananas. There was even one with a sewing machine.

Several times I noticed bare-breasted young girls wearing colourful wraps as a skirt, a piece of material covering their hair, and their faces and naked torsos painted white. Ironically some had made lace-like figures in the paint, so they seemed to be wearing a white lace blouse, complete with a low cleavage. 'An old tradition, sir, those girls are ready to be married off; they are being prepared for it by old women in the bush. During that time, they are painted white, are not allowed to look at the sea, and have to eat special food only. There is a shameful negative implication our government is fighting but with great difficulties. Those old witches in the forest are ritually deflowering the poor girls with a tool, and then they cut away the clitoris. It's a primitive, inhumane old tradition based on the macho assumption that the pleasures of sex should be the exclusive prerogative of the male of the species. It is now considered a crime, but we do not have the right to call ourselves a civilized society as long as those terrible abuses continue.' Lionel sounded embarrassed and ashamed.

Greenville appeared to be a smaller place than Buchanan, but quite similar. We drove through it but continued. Our next stop would be Barclayville, a tiny, mainly agricultural township of a few thousand people. We were now entering less developed areas of the country, and some parts of the road were in such bad condition that it was almost impossible to continue. Several times we pulled ourselves out of deep mud holes with the winch's hook around a tree trunk.

The third time it happened, I was just about to put the cable around a tree when a gunshot from behind startled me; I automatically ducked. Behind me stood Lionel with a revolver in his hand pointing at a thick branch. But the branch was no branch at all; it was a very dead snake, its head a bloody mess.

'Black Mamba, sir, absolutely deadly and aggressive too, thank God I noticed.' It would not be the last time Lionel saved my life.

When we finally reached Barclayville, it was almost dark, and as you know, darkness comes fast in the tropics."

But Harry did not have a clue. His mind's eye still saw a deadly black snake with a bloody shattered head that nearly killed him.

"There was no hotel in the township, but there were catholic and evangelical compounds, and we found a clean room for each of us there and a surprisingly tasty meal. My offer to pay was politely refused, but a donation to the mission was welcome. The small community lived from rice planting, growing vegetables and herding cattle. Due to the presence of the mission, there were a few good schools. We were tired and went to bed early. In the middle of the night, a clattering noise woke me up; a heavy downpour rattled on the corrugated metal roof. It did not last long, and I quickly fell asleep again, but I could imagine what the deluge would do to the jungle roads.

The next morning, I knew.

There were deep puddles on the road, in the field and all over the area. Patches of red and ochre-coloured mud soiled the lower part of the building. It was sticking to the bare-footed people's legs and to the few vehicles that drove by. A couple of pigs happily rolled in it. Everything that could hold water, empty barrels, buckets, wheelbarrows, clay pots, and hollowed-out tree trunks were overflowing. 'We better sit it out a couple of hours, sir,' Lionel advised, 'no use trying to get through this stuff, sir. The sun and the thirsty soil will do a good job on it. In a few hours, most of the water will be gone.'

It took a little bit longer, but at noon we decided to give it a try. The first part was the worst, we thought, because the coastal plane was lower. Zwedru is on the East side of the country, close to the border of the Ivory Coast and surrounded by thick tropical forest. We slipped and slid through parts of the muddy road, sometimes ending up in the ditch, but Lionel had done this before. At small settlements along the road, the downpour was a blessing for young kids. They deepened the part of the road that passed their adobe huts, forming a sizeable muddy water pool.

Cars would get stuck in it, and of course, we did too, which was precisely the intention. A whole group of half-naked young kids of all ages pushed us through while laughing, shouting and screaming, and we paid each one a dollar. There were two more of those 'expensive' toll-barriers ahead of us before we reached Zwedru; it made me laugh and the kids happy. There was not much to experience really in Zwedru. There had been a thriving lumber and wood processing industry, but not anymore. The surroundings were beautiful, and there were the most beautiful birds I'd ever seen. I already said that it was close to its neighbouring country, the Ivory Coast. That had some advantages. People from across the border came shopping, which helped the limited local economy. But there were problems too. French-speaking criminals would cross the border, commit a crime, and disappear before the local police could do anything.

It would be too late to continue our trip to Nimba, so we decided to stay in one of the small hotels, run by a friendly local couple, Ella and Stanley. They kept the place very neat and even offered two rooms with air-conditioning, at an extra charge. We took a refreshing shower and changed into something clean before we sat down at the veranda for a cool drink. 'Hey!' shouted Ella, who was dropping the two beers she brought; three men surrounded our Landrover. One was on the roof trying to get into a duffel bag.

Lionel was as quick as a tiger, he floored one of the men then turned to the second, but now I was there to join the fight and took the scoundrel in a chokehold from behind until he went down. The thief on the roof pulled a big knife, then blew a sharp whistle, and three other wolf pack members came running from behind the building. 'Come on,' whispered Lionel, who ran a few paces away from the car towards them. I understood and followed; he did not want to be jumped by the guy with the knife while fighting the attackers. The first two never knew what happened before they unconsciously hit the dirt. I knocked the third one down. Now the guy with the knife was off the roof, and one of the two robbers that Lionel knocked out first, was on his feet again, also with a knife in hand. 'Stay back, boss,' hissed Lionel. He took a few steps towards the couple and what happened next went so fast that I don't even know what he did, but both knives flew through the air, and the attackers were faced down on the ground, not making a move nor a sound. 'Can you open the car, please sir,' Lionel asked politely as if there were no six attackers sprawled around us. He took a bunch of flex handcuffs from his bag, and with my help, in no time, all six were detained and bound, still face down, side by side on the road. The hotel owners had called the police, and a noisy old police car arrived. Two officers jumped out, guns at the ready but quickly understood that the war had ended. Lionel showed them an ID, and they snapped handshakes, then slapped shoulders.

On our way to Nimba, Lionel told me the thieves formed a gang from Ivory Coast that raided the town from time to time. Then after disappearing in all directions, they could never be arrested.

The two brave officers would no doubt receive a promotion bringing all six in, he laughed.

Nimba was a relatively populous area for a country like Liberia, maybe some three to four hundred thousand people from different tribes, but mostly Dan and Mano. Nevertheless, the area is beautiful and worthy of becoming a natural park. There are diamonds and gold found in Nimba, timber and rubber and especially rich iron ore in Yekepa that a consortium of Bethlehem Steel and Sweden intended to exploit."

"So did you become a gold-digger again? Was that why you went to Liberia?" Harry asked.

"Hell no, I wasn't going to lose my money competing with the big boys there! Gold mining in Africa is either a big professional operation requiring lots of equipment or a very amateurish, low-paying venture. The pork-knockers there don't need competition from a white guy. They would kill me. Anyway, after Nimba, I thought I had seen enough of the country, so we went back to Monrovia. But first, I wanted to visit the Firestone rubber plantation in Harbel, south-east of the capital.

Vincent had given me a letter of introduction to the general manager of the enormous project,

George Vandalen.

14

Mr Vandalen was already aware of my visit. His great Liberian friend Vincent had informed him. 'Please come in, Bart, and it's George, not mister. You would, by the way, probably be the only one here pronouncing my name the way my dad did. He arrived from Holland between the First and Second World War and insisted on Van Dalen till the end of his life.'

George was in his mid-sixties. He seemed to be in good shape, had thick perfectly white hair, but the weathered skin of a man having lived his life in the tropics. We were sitting on the large veranda of his palatial white painted wooden house, which came as a fringe benefit to the demanding job. After exchanging pleasantries and accepting his invitation for dinner, George asked, 'So what brought you to Liberia of all places, Bart?'

I explained that I basically wanted to satisfy my curiosity, that I'd divested of my business interest in Alaska and would let life just happen. 'What about you?' I asked. He took some time to think. 'You know Bart, my wife passed away three years ago, she wasn't happy here anymore after both our sons went to college at home, in the States. She missed them terribly. I should have put in my resignation then. Still, things became very difficult with certain politicians here and with the union, so the board begged me to stay, and I did. I still regret it. I solved most of the problems, not all, but I'm burned out, and I resigned per the end of this year. I'm going home.'

George emptied his gin and tonic in one swig, then signalled to one of two servants in white uniform standing servile and silently against the wall, to bring him another.

'Don't get me wrong, Bart, many of the years I spent here were good. The country is beautiful and has great potential if they find a way to settle these damned tribal issues. I know exactly what I would do if I were younger.' The servant brought in two more drinks. Lionel had been served something cool in the car; he insisted on staying with it. 'What would that be then, George, if I may ask?'

'Sure, no problem. North of our place is an abandoned palm-oil plantation that once was a great producer. What happened, I don't know. Most of the buildings have been ransacked, the infrastructure is lacking maintenance and has been overtaken by the forest. Of course, trees need maintenance too, but the conditions here are ideal, and the palm trees are hardy. If I were younger, I would buy that plantation and bring it back to life. The price for palm oil is high and steady, and there is a great road now from here to the harbour of Monrovia; that's how we export our latex. It would ensure easy access to the world market.'

I thought about his words. *If anybody would know something about plantations, it was George Vandalen, the CEO of Firestone.*

'Why isn't there anybody in Liberia with that same vision, George?' I asked.

'There are several ways I could answer that question, Bart, but let me keep it nice and simple. It takes vision, capital, knowledge and entrepreneurship of a certain level and that combination is not readily available.'

'What if I was interested? Could you show me the way?' I said impulsively. 'Vision, capital and entrepreneurship I have, but I know nothing about running a palm oil plantation.'

'Are you serious?' George asked, looking surprised. He apparently never expected my reaction.

'Serious about looking at it, absolutely.' I replied.

'In that case, Bart, I suggest that you stay here till tomorrow, and we'll go and have a look at it. We have guest quarters for your driver, and you'll stay here. I do enjoy your company.'

After a royal breakfast the following day, Lionel drove the Landrover up, George insisted on sitting in the back. The abandoned old plantation was about three-quarters of an hour drive over reasonably good roads. The entrance gates must have been impressive once but were now just laying down, rusted and overgrown. We passed what once was the gate building, the road was still recognizable, but it was good we had our Landrover. On a large open square stood the ruins of the administrative buildings and warehouses. Everything that could be used, from doors and doorframes to corrugated roof sheets, floorboards, planks, pipes or taps, had been removed. It looked devastating. The stench of some dead beast, human and animal faeces and rotten fruit emanated from the debris. There was a junkyard of rusting demolished vehicles without wheels or tires. 'Forget about that rubbish, Bart, let's have a look at what counts here,' said George. We drove for miles on overgrown pathways cutting the plantation in large rectangular blocks divided into smaller squares planted with neat rows of mature palm trees. Many of them had dried-out bunches of fruit, and many showed large bunches with ripe orange kernels. The undergrowth covered the ground beneath the trees, ripe kernels must have dropped, and everywhere young shoots disturbed the neatness of the planted rows of mature trees.

'Here is your value, Bart, all those are mature fruit-bearing trees that will produce thousands of tons of produce each year. All that is required is to thoroughly clean up the place, fertilize with potassium and cow shit, easily obtainable here. Get rid of the varmints who feed on the ripe kernels, the snakes and other creepies and crawlies. Build new modern facilities, staff houses and accommodation for the workers, and purchase the latest machinery to reduce the number of workers. Put a fence around the main area and a guardhouse on both sides. You see, Bart, why there aren't many takers here? It's going to cost a bundle, but the global demand for palm oil is growing and is projected to do that for many years. It takes guts, but it could be very rewarding.'

We were standing next to our vehicle gazing at the almost

endless central wide road. A green snake as thick as my arm crossed some twenty yards in front of us, meandering at leisure as if to say, *my territory guys, watch it.* A group of monkeys protested loudly against our presence, and colourful birds were flying around or were feasting on the ripest kernels.

I liked what I saw.

'So what's next George, how do I go about it? Can you help me drafting a business plan and a budget? Do you know who to contact in the government to buy the place? Depending on the outcome of a feasibility study, I would like to buy the place and offer you a ten percent interest in the company we'll establish, for your advice, would that be OK?'

'Well, that was never my intention, but I accept if you put that interest in the name of my sons, and yes, I would actually enjoy the whole process; I have dreamed of it often enough.'

I spent three more days and nights at George's fantastic plantation house. We worked on a very detailed plan of operation, a budget and estimated revenues for the next five years.

It appeared highly profitable on paper, but the investment was significant, almost three million dollars, including a generous allocation for unforeseen expenditures. There would be some dues payable and some hands to be greased – an unavoidable nuisance – but nothing would be approved without it.

The ten percent allocated to both of George's sons, five percent each, was quite adequate for all their father's advice and hands-on assistance. He introduced me to the government officials able to sign the documents, and indeed, some payments were expected, but it was not too much. The company I established, BAROILIB LTD., did not become the owner of the land but received a ninety-nine-year irrevocable lease, paying no tax until the investment was recouped and after that a ten percent tax on the value of goods shipped. George introduced me to a tall Liberian, who was an engineer with years of experience at Firestone, whom I hired as general manager of my plantation.

What else is there to say, Harry? It became an enormous success.

It took nearly a year to clean the place, build all the buildings I needed, and create a new plantation home for the owner, which by the way, a young architect from Monrovia designed, and I loved it. After that, I imported the latest equipment and hired staff and workers. Fourteen months after I first talked to George, we were harvesting the first oil kernels. I bought four mobile machines that shook the ripe kernels from the tree, which increased production because we did not harvest green nuts anymore, and it took a lot fewer labourers.

Now I guess you do not know much about palm oil, so let me explain. The palm trees we have in Liberia are the *Elaeis guineensis,* good producers. The thick kernels are reddish-orange when ripe; the meat *mesocarp* becomes a sort of pulp that becomes oil. So there are two kinds of palm oil, reddish oil made from the pulp and white oil made from the hard kernels. In Africa and Asia, they use palm oil mainly for cooking, but the industry uses it for food, soap, detergents and many other products. The kernels are shipped to importers who sell them to the industry. The raw oil is refined, filtered, bleached and deodorized, and traded as RBDPO (**R**efined **B**leached **D**eodorized **P**alm **O**il). But, of course, I did not know anything about that either.

After shipping the ripe kernels for a couple of years and making good money – as it happens, my investment had been paid back in the first year already – I thought about the whole process.

George had been gone at the end of the first year, but we stayed in touch a lot, and his sons were delighted with the payments I made to them. After consulting George, who contacted several large industrial users of RBDPO, l ordered equipment from the United States to build a processing plant, and from then on, we only shipped the processed product. Our profits increased dramatically, and the price for our oil did too. I decided to invest in a significant expansion of the BAROILIB LTD., plantation, renegotiated the lease agreement with the government to change it into full ownership at additional payment, and built our own warehouse in the port of Monrovia. In hindsight, I overextended myself, but success with ventures you started can become addictive. I was happy, healthy and wealthy, and the plantation ran like a well-oiled machine.

But then something happened.

Lionel gradually became much more than a bodyguard. He was an intelligent man, and his way of dealing with people positively influenced our workforce. We paid our workers well, but it was the positive atmosphere that kept the labour and union problems Firestone had to deal with, outside our gate. Then, one fateful Saturday morning, Lionel said, 'Boss, I need to talk to you.' I realized that something serious was on his mind from the way he addressed me.

'Sir, I am afraid that your life may be in danger. There is something brewing among the people in this country that may result in armed insurrection against the government. It did not start here, but our people will inevitably be involved, as will those of Firestone.'

'Are you sure, Lionel?' I said, 'A revolution?', hardly comprehending what I heard.

'Yes, sir, I am. Some of our men are receiving instructions from Nimba, where the action committee is located. Because of our good relationship and in the strictest confidence, they told me that it could happen any day now. They told me they would not harm you, but once violence starts, others may. Therefore, sir, I regret to have to advise you that for your safety, you should take the first plane leaving Monrovia, and I urge you not to wait a day longer than necessary. I am sorry, sir.'

I was hoping the information was a bit too pessimistic, but Lionel was adamant, so I followed his advice. I told nobody about the fact that I was leaving, so I left behind written instructions. There was a flight to New York the next day, and I was fortunate to book the last ticket in first class.

While Lionel drove me to the airport, he told me not to worry too much; he would look after my interests until I could return, but of course, I was worried like hell. All my money was tied up in the place."

Bart took off his cap, scratched his head with a worried expression on his face, as if he just boarded the plane, leaving his plantation behind.

"What happened?" Harry asked, holding his breath, "Was he right, that Lionel, or was it just gossip? Did you go back later?"

"No, I didn't. It turned out that Lionel was entirely right, but the warning came almost too late. He drove me to the airport very early, so I would not miss my flight. When we were about an hour from Monrovia, two armed men were suddenly on the road in quasi-military outfits, pointing very realistic guns at us, signalling us to stop. 'Don't speak, sir,' Lionel whispered.

He stopped the car and got out, his hands half above his head. I could not overhear the conversation, but the men were pointing at the vehicle. Lionel moved very slowly, a bit closer to them. He retrieved a wallet from his pocket and held it up. What happened next went unbelievably quickly. He dropped the wallet, and in the same movement, grabbed the gun from one of them, shot the other, then cracked the skull of the first one with the butt of the weapon. He threw the gun down, got in the car, and we continued as if nothing happened. 'Bunch of amateurs,' Lionel said. 'Those are the kind of assholes that would have killed you, sir. I guess the shit has started.'

He was right again. A certain Samuel Doe from Nimba was

the leader, and he overthrew the government. I could never go back, the country became too dangerous a place, and Samuel Doe, in turn, was later cruelly murdered. I lost everything. All I had left was some money in Australia that I almost had forgotten about. I went back to Amsterdam, rented an apartment downtown and was drunk for a week, but that was not the way to solve problems.

I got hold of myself, transferred some money to the ABN-AMRO bank here, then I called Paisley in Anchorage. She was excited to hear from me, I'd kept in touch, but over time it had watered down. So anyway, she decided to come over; that's the kind of a friend she was.

Shortly after, I received news that shook me to the core. In a bloodthirsty frenzy, a group of drugged-up rebels raided my plantation, ransacked and burned the place, and murdered Lionel, Samuel, my CEO, and several staff members. I was devastated to lose my fortune, yet what pained me more was the death of these incredible, faithful men.

But what was I going to do with the rest of my life?

It was wonderful to see Paisley again. She still looked great and jumped in my arms at the airport. 'Howdy, sailor,' she said, then kissed me, holding on to me, and much of my pain disappeared. Then, back in my apartment, having a drink, I told her my whole story, 'But what about you, Paisley?' I asked, 'How's your life, any suiter I should kill? Are you still helping your dad out?'

'No lover to kill, sailor, unless you want to commit suicide. And, no, my Dad finally understood that he needed a permanent professional helper, so I finally finished my doctorate in anthropology.'

'So, what are your plans now?' Paisley asked that night, leaning back in the pillows cuddling up close to me after we'd exhausted ourselves. 'Are you staying in Holland?'

I told her I thought about it but that I decided to go to Suriname. That large island has a long Dutch history and...."

"Suriname is not an island, Bart. What are you talking about?" Harry was surprised. "Where did that come from? I had two guys from Suriname working for me, and they talked a lot, so I know. Suriname is in South America and definitely not an island. They were not the most diligent of workers but fun to be with, always laughter, always music, always fun. Raymond especially was a clown, he claimed he could fart the national hymn, and you would doubt him at your peril.

He would hide behind the bushes, particularly when a young couple strolled by, and then when they were close, he'd rip one that echoed through the park, just to see the embarrassed faces of the young lovers.

'I can't help it, boss,' he would say. 'It is my wife Lillian cooking that BB met R (brown beans and rice). 'You're pulling my leg, Raymond,' I said, but he answered, 'No. It's true, boss, wanna pull my finger?"

Then the two old storytellers both guffawed.

A mowing machine driven by a corpulent man half asleep, cutting the grass in front of them, made an ear-shattering tumult.

Both men kept silent. Suddenly with the narrative connection disrupted, something of the mystic was gone, and Harry moved subconsciously a bit away from the very verbal stranger. But with his hearing, especially in his left ear, very bad, he moved closer again not to miss a word when the mower passed, and Bart continued.

"So Paisley said to my surprise, 'Can I come along, Bart? I know there is lots to see for a brand new anthropologist in the Guianas, and I can pay my own way.' I said, 'Of course you can, I would love you to come with me, but you don't pay anything. I lost a fortune, but I am not completely broke yet.' So after showing Paisley Amsterdam, dining in some of the excellent restaurants, taking a boat ride through the canals encircling the old town, visiting the Rijksmuseum and the Van Gogh museum, I booked two tickets with the KLM to Paramaribo, the capital of Suriname."

15

"Why didn't you go by boat?" Harry quipped, "Didn't you say Suriname was an island?"

"Smartass", Bart retorted, "Do you want to hear my story or not? A man can make a mistake, you know, especially if you travelled as much as I did.

Anyhow, we landed at an airport in Suriname called Zanderij, which means something like 'sand-place', and I could see why! All around the airport were large areas of fine sand, as white as salt, but all around that was thick rainforest. It apparently was all natural, but it seemed like a giant circle was cut out of the jungle and sprayed from heaven with salt, an extraordinary sight. We took a taxi to the city, a ride of less than an hour. We passed adobe huts with little black kids playing around the house while mothers sold bananas, mangos and boiled eggs from improvised stalls on the side of the road. It was a bumpy ride, a heavy tropical downpour had made deep holes in the road, but the asphalt was in good condition closer to the city. The first houses in the periphery were unpainted and built with wide, roughly sawn boards on concrete columns and rusted corrugated sheets on the roof. There were usually a few fruit trees and tall banana plants around the house and a clean-swept sandy open place in front of it. Some larger constructions in the same style held Chinese general merchandise and grocery stores.

Closer to town, the houses were often well designed, solidly built homes, painted in pastel colours, with glass shutters and well-maintained gardens in front, bougainvillea climbing against the walls.

We passed the riverside with its monumental colonial buildings, across from them a large marketplace on the riverbanks, the old centre with its beautiful Dutch seventeenth-century buildings, then we reached our destination, Hotel Torarica.

The hotel was excellent and on a visually attractive site along the Suriname River. Anthropologist Paisley watched the people of Indian, African, Chinese, Asian and Dutch descent living together in harmony, with interest.

For some mysterious reason, they also drove on the wrong side of the road, like the Aussies.

So rather than killing ourselves, I rented a car with a driver to show us the country. To be honest, the city of Paramaribo was by far the most interesting. Although a modern town by any standards, it kept much of its seventeenth-century character in layout, architecture, and botanical variety. But the diversity and contrasts made it fascinating. There were men and women dressed in the latest fashion, and elderly women in traditional kotos, reminding one of the history of slavery, black professors and barefoot Ndyuka's in cotton wraps, Cadillacs and donkey carts, majestic tropical houses juxtaposed with the slave quarters still in the backyards. Modern office buildings, general stores with warehouses, colleges and clubs, banks and businesses of all sorts were in disharmony with the architectural beauty of historic buildings. The whole inner city is a World Heritage site, but how much longer?

For Paisley, it was heaven. She took many pictures, made notes and talked to almost everybody she met. Her charm, but especially the friendly attitude of the Surinamese people, made that easy. Surprisingly, she even received invitations to go and visit homes, which she did in some cases. As I'm sure you know, the official language in Suriname is Dutch, but most people speak English fluently, so Paisley had no problems.

We took a boat trip to see something of the interior and chartered a long dugout with a large new Evinrude outboard engine. A young black with a muscular naked torso was the engine driver while his father, who sat on the bow, gave him directions with hand signals or a stick. The dugout flew upstream through the water, with the old man in front pointing at obstacles like boulders, floating debris or shallow spots. Sometimes a dugout coming from the opposite direction flew by, carrying a dozen or so people and their belongings.

We were in awe of the beauty of the wild river, the jungle vegetation on its banks and the myriad of colourful birds, red and blue parrots with long tail feathers flying over our heads or monkeys among the trees, complaining about the intrusion of their world. Naked black children in a shallow part of the river, their wet little bodies shining as if freshly polished, laughing and waving at us.

If this was not paradise, it certainly came darn close. Until the late eighteen-hundreds, there had been more than a hundred plantations, producing sugar, coffee, tobacco and more, feasible during slavery times, but abandoned after abolition. The colonial history of Suriname as part of the Kingdom of the Netherlands shamefully includes many accounts of unthinkable cruelties, despite the attractive built environment of the capital and of some of the remaining palatial planter's residences. Some plantation owners, and especially their overseers, were despicable sadists and often murderers.

To understand the past and the present, we wanted to visit a few of those abandoned plantations. Not thinking of the possibility of reviving some, but rather to place the dramatic events of the past in a believable historical setting. I knew already from Indonesia and especially from Liberia that if you do not continuously fight the jungle, it rapidly overgrows everything you built, reclaiming what you took from it, healing the wounds you caused.

But two plantations were still recognizable as the large undertakings they once must have been.

The infrastructure, canals, bridges, and ducts were in shambles, and the main house was ransacked and unlivable. But many of the slave quarters and officer dwellings were now occupied by people living off the land and the river. On one, a large bronze bell which was used to call the slaves off the land was still hanging on what eerily resembled gallows. It was like the misery and pain, and the tears of generations of abused human beings had infused the overgrown soil we were walking on. A hallowed ground their broken bodies once tilled and planted so that the master would prosper. The ghosts of thousands of exploited fellow men, women, and children were tangibly hovering about, still not daring to leave the place that once owned their soul.

Paisley's tears flowed freely, and I just could not speak nor swallow.

On the way back to town, we were mostly quiet, still emotionally drained. It is one thing to know that slavery existed, but to stand right there on the lands where the stolen Africans suffered, is another. To sense the hidden graveyards of the ones that survived after being stacked on top of each other, shipped by Dutch vessels built for the purpose, accepting a twenty-five percent loss during transportation of the merchandise, it is all so tragically real walking there."

Both old men on the bench kept quiet as if the guilt of their forebears weighed on them as original sin. It was Harry who spoke first.

"When Hanna was five, she became very sick, and we had to take her to the hospital in South. The doctor who treated her was a black man from Aruba, and the nurse who cared for my little daughter as her own was from Ghana. The doctor and the nurse were the sweetest people I ever met, and when after six days we could take our child home, she cried when saying goodbye to them.

It was Anna, who was always smarter than me, who said that evening, 'Can you imagine how proud their great-great enslaved grandparents would be, knowing what became of those descendants?'

'For what?' I said, 'For treating white children?'

'No, dumbo,' Anna responded, 'for becoming nurses and doctors and for knowing no difference. For them, a child is a child. And when they go home at night, riding public transportation, you would be surprised by how many people would look down on them, thinking *'those are living off our welfare'*. Discrimination is a cancer, Har, for which there is no real medicine yet, but we should teach our children better.'"

"We didn't stay long in Suriname," Bart picked up his narrative, "not that we did not like the country, on the contrary. Paisley wanted to go to the interior to visit the Wayanas and Arawaks and other Indian tribes still living in the deep forest and the Amazon basin. To be honest, I liked the busy city better, but I understood and went with her anyway. After a couple of weeks, I don't remember exactly, while having a drink at the Torarica bar, we met a gentleman by the name of LeBlanc. He told us that incredible things were happening in neighbouring French Guiana, where Charles De Gaulle was building a missile base at a place called Kourou.

After booking a hotel in Cayenne, the capital of French Guiana, we took a taxi to Albina, a Surinamese hamlet on the wild Marowijne river with its many rapids. From there, we crossed the river to Saint Laurent on the French side. Saint-Laurent-du-Maroni, as it is officially called, is a small village that originally was not more than a French military settlement, but it expanded and in character, it resembled a small village in France.

To be honest, we were not very interested in the construction of a missile base. Still, we knew of Devil's Island off the coast of Kourou, where so many French political prisoners of the second French Empire perished. Prisoners from all over the French Empire were sent to Saint Laurent. From there, they were shipped to Devil's Island. It was developed in 1852 as a penal colony, and the place became infamous for its harsh treatment – as many as seventy-five percent of the inmates would die there. It closed only in 1953. I read the famous story about the French captain Alfred Dreyfus, who was sent to that penitentiary for life, wrongfully accused of treason, in reality, just because he was Jewish. I also read the autobiography of Henri Charrière, a French writer who, accused of murder, was sent to Devil's Island and spectacularly escaped. His book *Pappilon* was made famous by Dustin Hoffman, who played Charrière in the movie of that name, so I wanted to see the place."

"I saw that movie, together with Anna, in the Alhambra theatre," Harry said, sounding surprised. "Are you telling me that really happened and was not just a story?"

"You better believe it, I have been there. I saw the ruins of the buildings, the holes in the ground closed off with iron bars where prisoners were kept like animals—a dreadful place.

Anyway, there was a restaurant in Cayenne," Bart resumed, "where we liked to go and have a glass of wine on the shaded terrace. An elderly man, slovenly dressed in a suit two sizes too big for his frail body, peddled a book called *Après l'enfer,* that's French, it means *After the hell*. He was one of the survivors, a political prisoner who, after so many years in hell, spent his last years hawking his written misery. I still have the book.

It was at the same place, that we ate for the second time, a portion of delicious large fresh shrimps, baked in garlic butter, served with a toasted baguette. 'Where do you get these fantastic shrimps from?' I asked the waiter. 'From the fishermen, monsieur, they bring them in every morning.' I decided to go and have a look at the harbour early next morning while Paisley stayed at the hotel to work out some of her drafts.

There were several boats that brought their catch in, which was mainly bought by local individuals and restaurant owners. I started talking with one of the fishermen who thankfully spoke English; my French was a bit rusty. What I learned from him was that the waters in front of French Guiana held massive amounts of nutrients for the large shrimps they were catching.

The man I talked to claimed that within an hour, he could catch more than he could ever sell, and it was the same with the other boats.

Back in the hotel that evening, his words kept spinning

through my head. The shrimps were extraordinarily tasty, and I was convinced I would find a willing market abroad. But it would need quite a bit of investment, a processing plant to clean and pack the shrimps, a freezer warehouse, an ice-making facility for the fishing boats to keep their larger catch fresh, and so on. I did not sleep much that night.

The next morning, I called George, who was happy to hear from me and stated again how sorry he was about my losses. When I explained what my plans in French Guiana were, he asked if I would accept him and his sons as a twenty-five percent partner. They would come in with finance and could handle the logistics in the United States because he was convinced that there would be a massive market if the prawns were as good as I said. We decided that the best thing for him to do was to come to Cayenne and see for himself, which he did.

Paisley observed that evening, 'I see you're dreaming big again, sailor. Time for me to go back to Alaska where I will accept a teaching job unless you go down on your knees right now and put at least five carats on my finger'. She laughed because she wasn't serious. I think we loved each other as friends, and both would not let marriage spoil a beautiful thing, so she left.

George was scheduled to arrive three days after Paisley's departure, so in the meantime, I went to the missile base in Kourou to pay a visit to the man in charge of transportation.

As I correctly assumed, twice a week, a chartered cargo plane, a modified Lockheed Galaxy, brought general cargo to Cayenne for the missile base project. It would return virtually empty to Fort Lauderdale. When I asked if it would be feasible to negotiate a contract for a weekly return cargo, the man was very enthusiastic because it would benefit both.

When George arrived, we paid a shrimper to take us on board, so at 5 a.m., we were out at sea, and an hour later, our nets were full; most of the catch were large prawns.

We had our answer.

The next thing to do was basically administrative; we needed to form a company after assuring the government's cooperation. There was a maître notaire in the city who was of great help in preparing all the documents in French and English and in obtaining the necessary government licenses. He even negotiated a five-year tax exemption for our new company, BARGEO *Fruits de la Mer Sarl.*

George went back home, and his experience as a top manager showed. In only a few weeks, the company was registered in the U.S.A., a bank account was opened, and a line of credit was established. I transferred a quarter of a million dollars to our U.S. account and a hundred thousand to Credit Agricole in Cayenne. We rented sufficient space at the harbour to build our facilities, and since the harbour was government property, the terms were very reasonable.

Within four months, we built the freezer warehouse, the cleaning and packing plant, the ice maker for the boats, an administrative building and a building for the employees, all from pre-fabricated elements sent from the U.S.A. One of George's sons, and a shareholder, of course, took care of designing the boxes, which each would contain 60 large shrimps, 24 of those would go in a foam box and 40 of these on a pallet. In addition, George had been able to hire six women from Thailand for half a year to teach the mostly female employees how to clean, sort and pack the shrimps.

Before we officially opened the plant, we processed large quantities, most of which needed to be destroyed before the process was efficient, sanitary, and faultless.

George had been able to gain interest from a food-wholesale company with cold storage facilities in Miami to import and distribute whatever we could ship. They sent a quality controller who would permanently stay in French Guiana, then finally, the day was there.

Our official opening was a big event. The mayor of Cayenne arrived, representatives from the business community, the CEO of the company who was going to import the prawns, even several officials from the missile base, the press, and of course George and both his sons.

It was an unusual hour for a festive event, 8 a.m., but we wanted the visitors to watch the whole process, and we could not delay bringing the catch in much later. It was a great success, and the papers wrote about the positive effect our company would have on the fishermen, our employees and ultimately the country's economy.

We started with three boats, but within a year, that number doubled, and two years after we started, we were able to keep twelve boats busy. Of course, we had to expand the freezer capacity, but that was all, and luckily the missile base needed two flights per week, which suited us perfectly. This time I stayed with the company and in French Guiana for five years. I made a fortune again, when agreeing with George, who was getting old and tired, to accept the offer from the company that imported our prawns. It netted me seven and a half million dollars."

"Are you kidding me?" Harry said, "From shrimps? Nobody can be that lucky, Bart. First, the gold, the lumber, then the palm oil – I know you lost all that again. But how fortunate can a guy be? I have never met a millionaire in my life, and you make it sound like, I don't know, like it was so damned easy, while I was breaking my back just to support a family."

Harry sounded like he was convinced that life had thrown him a curveball and that all the luck providence bestowed on humanity had landed on that sailor next to him with his incredible stories.

"Then what happened?" he asked, in a voice that wondered why the almighty could not have redirected his blessings, just for once. But he wanted to hear it all.

16

"I had been on the road for so many years that I realized there would come a time that I had to settle down. And the older you get, the more intense the feeling that you want to belong somewhere. You start idealizing the country of your youth because you are ignorant of all the negative changes progress caused there. You start longing for those years when life was simple, the world small, and your ambitions still underdeveloped. I decided to go back to Holland and find myself a nice house to my liking so that even if my wanderlust appeared not yet dead, there would always be someplace in the world waiting for me, someplace I could call home. I have always considered Amsterdam my hometown, so I booked a suite in the Amstel Hotel to give myself time to find what I wanted. It took less than three weeks. After considering many options, I found the place of my dreams, a stately merchant house on the Heerengracht, with for the inner city, a surprisingly beautiful backyard. The owner was an elderly Jewish gentleman who reminded me of an emaciated Atlas, carrying the world on his shoulders. He was not tall and could be either sixty or eighty because although his face betrayed his seniority, his eyes had a youthful, intelligent spark. I took an immediate liking to him. He invited me to come inside his richly appointed home, furnished with valuable antiques, expensive paintings, and many old black and white pictures in silver frames. They seemed to be well-to-do people, some of them wearing a yellow star on their coats. *What was this sympathetic lonely old man doing in this large, four-story seventeenth-century merchant's home?* He seemed to read my mind. 'You may wonder why I am living all by myself in so large a building. I can tell you if you are interested, but bear with me; it is a long and sad story.' I answered that I had all the time in the world and that I was very interested. 'From the documents we signed, you already know that my name is Jacov Mandelbaum and that I am obviously Jewish. Many generations before me, my predecessors came to Amsterdam after escaping the pogroms of Southern Europe, benefitting from the humane laws in the Netherlands. The tolerant country offered citizenship to Jews, allowing us to practice our religion, build synagogues, participate in economic activities, education, sciences and cultural events. It was unprecedented in the Europe of those days. Our name has not always been Mandelbaum. We are Sephardic Jews, which means we originate from Sepharad, the Hebrew name for Spain and Portugal. At the end of the fifteenth century, my family was expelled from Portugal. Being welcomed in what was then called the Low Countries – when The Netherlands and Belgium were still one – we adopted a new family name. The first Portuguese-Spanish synagogue was built in Amsterdam. Abraham Cohen

Pimentel was the Rabbi; he died in 1697. It may surprise you, but that synagogue is still in use today and services are still held in Portuguese, that is, if there is a minyan.

Where are my manners?' Mr Mandelbaum suddenly changed the subject, 'I did not offer you a drink, my apologies. What can I offer you, do you like wine? I have a nice Cabernet Sauvignon from the Tura mountain, it is Kosher, but you won't taste that.' There was a sparkle in his eyes and a thin smile on his face. Then, after pouring us both a glass, the old man continued.

'We both profited and prospered, this country and the Sephardic Jews. We brought our trading expertise and global connections, navigation knowledge, and techniques. The Netherlands started to compete with Spain and Portugal in overseas trade.

There were artisans among us, merchants and many physicians, scientists and teachers, and wealthy entrepreneurs. We were loyal to the Dutch Republic and helped expand or establish Holland's influence in the East and the West. True, some professions were still anathema to us, like studying law, because we could not take a Christian oath. Nor could we become members of the guilds, but other than that, we thrived. Some excelled, like Menasseh Ben Israel and Baruch Spinoza, whose names I am sure you know.

L'chaim,' Mr Mandelbaum toasted, 'To life.' I reciprocated his toast, 'and to your health, sir.' Mr Mandelbaum swirled the dark red wine in his glass, took a sip, smacked his lips, then continued.

'But Jews never take life for granted, so when in 1794 French troops marched into the South Netherlands, the Jewish population in the north, especially those in Amsterdam, were worried. Our beloved Prince of Orange had been expelled. Surprisingly whatever limitations still applied to the diaspora in this country, then known as The Batavian Republic, our condition significantly ameliorated. In 1796 The National Convention even proclaimed an un-comprehensible resolution of the following text:

No Jew shall be excluded from the rights and advantages which are associated with citizenship in the Batavian Republic, and which he may desire to enjoy.

Moses Asser became a member of the court of Justice, and Moses Moresco was appointed a member of the municipality of Amsterdam. Henceforth our congregations received grants from the treasury just as indeed the Christian congregations did. Our respect for the House of Orange was recognized by following generations in the Kingdom, Amsterdam in particular. But Holland, in general, was a major centre for the Jewish population and contributed significantly to the prosperity that followed. Even today, the spoken language in Amsterdam still contains a cornucopia of colourful expressions that are of Jewish origins, such as;

Gabber (friend)

Mesjogge (crazy)

Gein (fun)

Penoze (underworld)

Schlemiel (sucker)

Mokum (Amsterdam)

Hundreds more maybe, and you know them all Bart, without realizing their Jewish origin. Amsterdam was such a fantastic liberal, fun and safe place to live for us. We had a home, Jerusalem of the North, they called it.

Until the unthinkable happened.'

Mr Mandelbaum, who told me to call him Jacov, which I could not bring myself to do because he emanated that much respect, took another sip of his wine. But I noticed his hand slightly shaking when he put the glass down.

'My great-grandfather Baruch was a spice trader, not big but successful enough to support his family and the synagogue. My grandfather, standing on the shoulder of his Abba, may his soul rest in peace, turned what he inherited into one of Amsterdam's largest spice trading companies. He bought the house that I am now living in and have just sold to you, praying you will respect its history. Zayde, my grandfather, made sure all his seven children would have a good education and respect and practice our Jewish religion. My Abba, the third child, became a doctor, graduating from the Erasmus University in Rotterdam. When my grandparents passed away and were buried in Ouderkerk, my Abba inherited the house where he lived happily with his bride. It had been a matchmaker-arranged marriage with Havvah, my wonderful loving mother. But my father did not practise his profession from this prestigious merchant's house. Instead, he could be found in the poorest parts of the city, where children walked barefoot, malnourished and unwashed. The families there lived in dire circumstances in uninhabitable hovels in slums the sun never touched. Yet everybody, whether Jew or Christian, knew '*Doctor Mandel*' who always helped and never charged.

We lived off the few wealthy patients my father treated, but I was the oldest with three sisters and two brothers, so there were never any extras. Mother never complained; she explained to us that we were so much better off than the poor children our Abba tried to help. But the Sabbath was warm, and when we received the blessing, we felt the light of the candle warming our hearts, as much as the Sabbath meal did. I never received an expensive education, but Adonai bestowed his blessings on me; I had a good brain and sjoege.

Then a dark shadow fell over Europe.

Some of us saw it coming and left for Switzerland, or America but soon, all borders in the '*Free*' world were closed to us. Many more did not believe it or comprehend it; much of the stories they heard or read were too gruesome to be true. Then the razzia's started, and thousands of good law-abiding people were herded like animals, beaten into cattle cars, and transported to their deaths. They were told they'd be going to workcamps and received a list of what to bring, so how bad could it be? One day this also would be over.

Tolerant Holland was hiding too many anti-Semitic scoundrels among all social levels of its citizens. Some did not even understand the term but were quite willing to sell the hiding place of an entire Jewish family to the Nazis or the collaborating Dutch police in return for fifteen Guilders per head or to avoid having to pay back the debt they owed to the people they betrayed.'

It was very silent in the room. A grandfather clock in the hallway chimed; Mr Mandelbaum's breathing was short. He just stared at the distance, his eyes getting moist, but all the tears a human body holds had been shed already many years ago. Then his eyes wandered over the framed pictures on the wall. Way too many.

'But allow me to leave it at that, Bart, the memories are too painful, and the unthinkable cannot be explained. My whole family was murdered. I am the sole survivor. How I survived, I don't know, but I did. Maybe it was the realization that somebody had to stay alive in order to tell the world. Still, when I came back as one of the few survivors, the world was not interested. Did I know how bad *they* had it in Holland during the German occupation?

Sometimes I have a nightmare, and it all comes back; at other times, it is as if it never happened, then I look at the tattooed number on my arm, and I know.

When I finally arrived in Amsterdam, to go to my parents' home, I found out that it had been sold. How could that be? Bought from whom? I soon found out.

Friends of Hannah Knopfnagel, the woman who betrayed us, had moved into our house only days after we were deported, so it was not only the Judas pieces of silver that made her do it. In 1943 she *'fell'* in a canal and drowned. But the family who now lived in our home had obtained legal ownership, according to the post-war Dutch legal system, that all too often deprived Jews guilty of surviving, of their possessions.

There were some people who remembered doctor Mandel and his altruism, and they were shocked to hear about the murder of the family; they offered to help me get back on my feet. Not knowing what to do, I decided to start selling spices like my great grandfather, but on a very small scale. What else is there to tell? Ultimately, I was as successful as he had been and became wealthy. When the person who occupied the house my father inherited died, I offered his widow through an intermediary a price she could not refuse, and I moved back into our family home.'

'But then why sell it, Mr Mandelbaum?' I asked him.

'A good question, Bart. I want to spend my remaining years in Israel. As you know, homes like this one are very much in demand. When I contacted a real estate agent, he responded with an offer much higher than the price I asked for and two hundred thousand Guilders more than you paid. I found out his client's name was Von Stauffer. An executive from Bayer Nederland, a derivative of IG Farben, the war-time producer of Zyklon B, the gas used to murder my people."

Both Bart and Harry remained silent for quite a while.

"Did you ever hear from him after he left for Israel?" Harry asked, breaking the silence.

"Yes, once he wrote me a letter, telling me he was at peace and finally home. He explained that he had carried a certain feeling of guilt in Holland – why did he survive when all his loved ones perished. That feeling was gone after he prayed for them at the Wailing Wall."

"Were you happy in that house?" Harry asked.

"Yes, I was, but not for long. I started to miss Paisley. Every now and then, at first, but gradually it became a longing. We called often, but that made things worse, so I decided to go to Alaska again. I listed the house with a rental agency, giving verbal instructions not to accept Germans, and for a period of twelve months only. After all, this is Amsterdam, and an empty house is soon broken into by squatters. So I packed a suitcase and took a taxi to Schiphol airport.

17

When I landed at Anchorage, much to my surprise, there was no Paisley welcoming me. Did she not receive my message, or was something wrong? It worried me.

Arriving at the cottage with the stables I'd bought her, a housekeeper opened the door, indicating to be quiet with a finger against her lips. Once inside, I subconsciously noticed how tastefully decorated her place was, and I smelled the fresh flowers on the coffee table.

'She fell in the stable, sir,' the housekeeper explained, 'She slipped over something and badly hurt her head. I called the doctor, and he came right away; she has a concussion, is what he said, and that she had to rest.'

Paisley was sleeping. There was no visible injury, but a concussion is something very dangerous if you do not take it seriously, so rest is what she was going to get, I would make sure of it. The cottage has a second bedroom, so I installed myself there. 'When did this happen?' I asked, and the woman told me, 'Day before yesterday, sir.'

I went to the stables to make sure somebody had taken care of the horses, the housekeeper told me there was a stable boy, but as if by a fluke, he had a week off to go and see his parents.

A dozen horses were staring at me when I entered, trotting restlessly around in their stable or kicking the boards, whinnying in protest that nobody fed them. The stables were neat and well organized. I first gave each horse an armful of hay and half a bucket of water, then a generous helping of grain. I knew that a horse's digestive system is delicate and rough fibers are needed to avoid a colic that can be deadly. It quieted the horses, and I swear they were smiling at me. There were two wheelbarrows and tools, so I cleaned the stalls, but first, I checked on Paisley, although she was still sound asleep. Feeding a dozen horses and cleaning stables is quite a job, especially if you are not used to it, so I was tired when it was done and went inside to take a shower and have a beer. When I sat in a comfortable chair, her Labrador dog cuddled up to me, wagging its tail, probably having decided that a guy smelling like a horse should be ok.

I checked on Paisley again, and by then, she was awake. With a soft voice but a twinkle in her eyes, she said, 'Hello sailor, taken care of the horses first, didn't you?'

'I can serve you a helping of hay any time, dear. How are you falling, eh feeling, I mean?'

'Feeling much better for seeing you. Didn't do great falling, though, but I don't intend to practice. How've you been, Bart?'

I told her, then I made some soup; she said she wasn't hungry, but I made her eat it. She still had a headache, so I told her to rest, then carefully closed the door behind me.

After three more days of rest, Paisley could not stay in bed any longer. She was still weak but feeling much better, and she missed her horses. The ungrateful monsters made a hell of a noise when she entered the stable, completely ignoring the person who'd fed them and cleaned the mess they made in their boxes. A man may like a horse, women fall in love with it, and the sentiment is reciprocated.

It was good to be with Paisley again. I realized how much I had missed her, her humour, her straightforward no bullshit attitude, and the love and comfort I found in her arms. There was no greeting more welcoming to me than her *'Howdy sailor'*, never without a smile and stars in her eyes.

'So, how's teaching?' I asked her one day.

'Gave it up, sailor. As much as I loved studying, teaching is not my thing.'

'So what do you do for a living besides pampering horses?' I asked.

'Come, let me show you.' she answered. So I followed her, she stopped in front of a box on the right. 'That is Midas,' she said, but I already knew, it was written on his stall. It was a nice young horse as far as I could tell, not large but well built. 'I just sold him. His new owner will come to get him next week after paying me two hundred and fifty thousand American dollars, sailor. So for the next couple of months, we should be alright unless you keep drinking those numbers of cold beer every afternoon,' she laughed.

'What? A quarter of a million for that horse? What does he do, tapdancing?'

'Almost,' she replied. 'Look at his hindquarters, how strong, that's his engine, and you see how broad his chest is? Great lungs on that one. He'll go to Argentina to be trained as a polo pony.

So you see, pampering a horse can pay off, easier than most men too, sailor.' She shoved me with her elbow.

'I read about polo,' I said, 'never saw a game, but are they using horses that are that expensive?'

'Oh yes, and much more expensive than Midas. Most players have a string of them; a game consists of four to six chukkers lasting seven minutes. For each chukker, the player uses a different horse and keeps half a dozen in reserve. There is a reason why it is called the king of sports and the sport of kings. For example, an Argentinian polo player and horse breeder owns a stallion named Aiken Kura. It made him many millions of dollars just from the semen that sold at more than one hundred thousand dollars per shot, and it will make much more when it retires from the game.'

'Christ, so I was cleaning royal shit the past couple of days. These horses represent a fortune.'

'Not that easy, Bart. You saw those mares in the other stable? Maybe one, if I am lucky, two may be good breeders. The one in stall five, maybe. If I receive the two-fifty, I may spend a hundred thousand on a shot of a famous stallion, and she may give me a winner, but that is not a sure thing. So yes, there can be good money in it, but it is a risky business. You will not believe the money that goes around in a country like Argentina in this sport, where Polo is as popular to the general public as soccer is in Holland. But mind you, it is played in more than fifty countries. Here in the USA, in England, Australia, Canada... but the horse culture in Argentina made the sport there exceptionally popular.'

'Have you been there, in Argentina, I mean?' I asked.

'No, not yet, but I plan to one day.'

'How could you leave? Those horses here are going to cry their heart out.'

'I know, they will,' she laughed, 'but my *stable boy* is in his thirties, very capable and extremely knowledgeable about horses. So I would leave my horses with him without the slightest concern.'

'When is he coming back?'

She looked at me, raising her eyebrows, 'What are you thinking about, sailor?' she said.

'Thinking of flying to Miami, from there to Buenos Aires, but don't worry, I'll send you pictures,' I answered.

'So you think you can come to Alaska to tell me that? Going to watch Argentinian polo without me? Now, who fell on his head, sailor, you or me? On your own, you'll end up in a soccer stadium or some house of ill repute, so let me ask you again, what are you thinking about, sailor?'

She looked quasi-serious at me, then we both laughed.

'How about it then?' I asked.

'Packing my suitcase in a bit, Bart, it is a crazy and wonderful idea. I sure need a break, and I don't mean of my skull. I could learn a lot and make some interesting contacts there. I believe the Hurlingham is on pretty soon.'

'Hurlingham?'

'The second most important polo event in Argentina after the Campeonato Argentino in Buenos Aires.'

'That's it then, Pais, I'll book the tickets and the hotel. After that, you make whatever arrangements are necessary to visit the right places and see the right people. By the way, what should I pack?'

'Chic-sportive for the polo events. I am a registered breeder, we'll be in the VIP section, and it will be a true fashion parade, but amicable with lots of champagne and caviar. I suggest we make a stop in Miami and go shopping; I certainly need a few things.'

What she meant by *'a few things'* I found out when we ended up with five suitcases instead of the two we had with us, leaving from Anchorage. We stayed three days in Miami, then boarded Aerolineas Argentinas for the nine-hour flight to the Ministro Pistarini Airport in Buenos Aires. The first class was very comfortable, and the service on board, excellent.

I had booked a suite in the traditional Alvear Hotel, a beautiful hotel built in the nineteen-thirties, situated in the upscale Recoleta neighbourhood. With an important tournament upcoming, I was lucky to even find a room, but low and behold, the bridal suite had been cancelled just one hour before I called, so we were lucky.

It was the first visit for both of us to Argentina and its capital. Naturally, we admired the neo-classical buildings that dominated the city. Argentina gained independence from Spain early in the nineteenth century, and pompous bronze statues of past conquerors on their steeds raised high above street level on marble pedestals were still at the centre of many a square or city park. To be honest, I did not know much about Argentina, but I was curious after the movie *Evita* and the emotional song *Don't cry for me Argentina*. Other than that, there were vague stories about many Nazi war criminals finding refuge in Argentina after the war while Juan Perón was president."

"Did you see any of them?" Harry interrupted, "I remember reading about it, how a lot of those Nazi animals escaped through Rome with the help of the Vatican to South America. There was a Pope then, called Pius, and some claimed that he made deals with top Nazis during the war so they would leave the Vatican in peace, I remember that."

"They did not exactly walk around with one of those high caps with a skull-and-bones insignia on their head. They were hidden in the fabric of the Argentinian society like cancer spreads among healthy tissue. Many became quite influential in business and the government, but let me finish my story.

So, it was a good thing we went shopping in Miami because in the hotel and in many restaurants, people still dressed what some may call conservative, but we both liked it. Then came the day we went to the Campo Argentino de Polo. We were going to watch the *Campeonato Argentino Abierto de Polo* and what an event it was."

In Amsterdam, the sun disappeared behind the tall trees; it was a quarter past three. Most mothers with children were getting their things together and prepared to leave the park. The two policemen on their bicycles returned, smiling at the old-timers still sitting on the bench as if they were on duty. The more Bart told, and the longer he talked, the better his memory seemed to become. Places, times, and events seemed to pop up like he learned the narratives by heart, and he seemed to master a handful of languages from the easy way he pronounced foreign names.

Harry was spellbound. He put his coat back on, not that it was necessary yet, but to indicate that he was ready to stay until sundown.

18

"You know the chaos when there is an important soccer tournament in Holland or a football game in America? Well, this is worse. Maybe chaos is not the right word because it is all very well organized. Still, an enormous mass of people needs to be seated; I guess fifty thousand, or even more. In most countries, polo is elitist, and the public are usually members of an exclusive polo club, not so in Argentina. There are different classes of seats for the games, from the most expensive to the cheapest in the high corners of the stadium. But that is where you find the real connoisseurs loudly commenting, advising, cheering or booing the players. They know the rules to the letter and have a favourite player that they idolize, with the name and their hero's high handicap number on a T-shirt.

The VIP section is an entirely different story. Once we passed through the security gates, in front of which numerous paparazzi were taking photos, we were welcomed by men in blue blazers with an impressive FIP (Federation International de Polo) logo on their left breast.

On the right of a large open area, where hundreds of fashionably dressed people were strolling, to see or to be seen, was a long row of nicely built stalls. They were staffed with beautiful girls, offering the most luxurious items from every corner of the world. On elevated platforms were the latest polished models of Rolls Royce, Ferrari, Bugatti and others. In a separate section and visibly presented, there were different models of German cars, Mercedes, BMW, Porsche and Audi.

On the left side of the plaza, where the private lodges were located, insurance companies, banks, breeders and private individuals welcomed anybody visiting, with the best champagne, caviar and hors d'oeuvres. Bodyguards trying hard not to look like bodyguards, kept an eye on ladies wearing what could be the crown jewels for a mid-size nation. Maybe a dozen languages were spoken. Yes, there was a good serving of snob-appeal, but it was clearly about polo and horses. Several of the riders walked around shaking hands. They were dressed in white riding breeches with knee-length leather boots and polo shirts with large handicap numbers on them, so spectators could see who was playing. The safety helmet on their head, with the loosened chin-protector hanging from the strap, they walked around like semi-gods.

Paisley was recognized by a gentleman, wearing a dark pink coat over white slacks, a turquoise silk kerchief in his breast pocket and a mismatched club tie. 'Paisley, dahlink,' he greeted her, with two kisses and only a slight Spanish accent, 'How have you been, and who is the lucky man?'

Paisley introduced me with a big smile, 'This is Bart, my

bodyguard, Rodrigo, so you better behave because he is deadly and very ill-tempered.' Rodrigo got the joke, smiled pearly white teeth from a light brown face at me, then shook my hand. 'Well, congratulations, a beautiful body to guard Bart,' he said laughing. 'Welcome to the games. Are you somehow involved in polo?'

'If you asked me that question tomorrow, Rodrigo, I could say yes. But right this moment, it is all very new to me.' I answered. 'This hippophile who brought me here insists that if I watch a polo game once, I'll be lost and a fan for the rest of my life.'

'Well, then allow me to introduce you to what keeps these events rolling, Cristal champagne, our booth is over there, you'll meet some nice folks. That ok with you, Paisley?'

While we were sipping champagne, shaking hands, kissing and being kissed, the noise from the packed stadium reached its crescendo. Paisley indicated that it was time to take our reserved seats in the VIP section, to watch the start of the first chukker."

"What is a chukker?" Harry asked.

"As I said before, the game is played in six short periods of seven minutes each; that's when the players change their horses to a fresh one. Those periods of seven minutes they call chukkers, but let me finish my story.

So there I was sitting, not exactly without means myself, among the wealthiest of the earth who'd flow in on private planes for thirty-six hours of what, in my eyes at the time, resembled field hockey from the back of a horse. At first, I felt ill at ease until Paisley insisted that my ivory coloured pants, the Ferragamo shoes, the light coat with its large blue and pink checkered pattern, the white open light-blue shirt, and the Panama hat, were just the right touch. Looking around me, I realized how right she had been.

What can I say about the game? I have to admit that I started to enjoy it. The corner enthusiasts helped me to understand, with deafening noise, when a rider did something great or committed a foul. The public was of the opinion that the mounted referee should call a penalty. I remember that the score ended in 12-10 but don't ask me who won. It must have been good, though, because the crowd was jubilant. Some of the VIP's were high-fiving or lifting their champagne glasses. In contrast, others in our section never even watched the game but instead were just chatting.

As it turned out, Rodrigo was a horse breeder; he was likeable but also a bit enigmatic. We accepted his invitation for dinner that night in one of the great local restaurants, where most of the tables were occupied by the same VIPs. Though now in different Chanel's, De La Renta's and Versace's. Paisley, looking stunning, dressed in something very expensive, received a few more kisses from men and jealous stares from women, whereas I was mostly ignored.

There was another couple at our table, a Klaus Von Schweringen and his charming Argentinian wife. Von Schweringen was also a horse breeder, so I felt a bit of an outsider at the table.

The conversation was amicable but mostly about horses. Noticing that I had been rather quiet, Von Schweringen asked, 'Tell me, Bart, what are you doing to justify the attentions of lovely

Paisley?' I did not really like the way he wanted to find out what I did for a living, but it was not an insult either. Men tend to do that; they want to know about the guy they are introduced to, like dogs sniffing each other before they decide to fight or play.

'To justify Paisley's attention, Klaus,' I answered, 'I clean stables, but if you are wondering what I do for a living, I own shopping malls in a number of European capitals.'

It was a nonsense answer, of course, but I wanted to trump Von Schweringen's rather arrogant behaviour. It silenced him, and I noticed a little smile on Paisley's face.

That evening back in the hotel, Paisley said, 'You put that Von Schweringen nicely down a peg; he is not a bad guy, though. Seems a bit arrogant, but it must be his upbringing because if you know him, he is quite nice, and they are great breeders.'

'So am I, baby, so am I,' I quipped, then she playfully hit me. 'How come these breeders can afford this lifestyle? I now know what you meant when you said so much money was involved. Is it that profitable?' Paisley took some time before she answered. 'There are so many false rumours about this business, those who never made it are claiming that it is great to make capital, provided you started with a fortune. But that is not true. On the contrary, most of those negativists were trying to get into it with not enough capital, so for them, it was bound for failure. If you have the means to invest properly, I mean millions, your success is almost guaranteed, and your return will be many times your investment.'

'How is that possible? How big can the demand be?' I ignorantly wondered aloud.

'Billions of dollars, mister shopping mall owner.' She assured me, 'Polo ponies from Argentina? Are you kidding me? Many an Arabian player would give the right arm of his servant for it. Some own a stable of several hundred, not one below half a million and many several million each. And, as I said, the game is the oldest team sport in the world and played in more than fifty countries.'

I was flabbergasted and did not fall asleep easily that night. I thought about my lumber, my palm oil, and the shrimps. I had lousy luck several times but seemed to have the ability to make a success of what I undertook. I guessed as much as I liked to think of myself as a sailor, I was more of an entrepreneur later in life than I ever intended to be. Should I get involved in the apparently lucrative business of polo pony breeding, with Paisley as an advisor? Then why would I? I fell asleep, deciding to let it rest.

The next day we went to Mendoza, where the famous Malbec wine is produced. A chartered Learjet took us there in two hours. There was no more talk about horses. Instead, it was more about wines, which I like to drink, but Paisley was more knowledgeable about. The private limo I had ordered was waiting on the tarmac to take us to our hotel, the *Cavas Wine Lodge*. There was another dream on Paisley's wish list; she liked to dance and wanted to visit a place were people danced the Tango. 'Tango?' the young driver asked, surprised, 'My grandparents used to dance that madam.

I can take you to a place where they dance the Macarena,' he laughed, but my queen was not amused.

We visited several vineyards and tasted the dark fruity wines made of the small Mendoza grapes. Paisley bought several cases she then had shipped to her father's place in Alaska.

Back in our hotel in Buenos Aires, there was a note with a phone number asking me to call; it was from Von Schweringen. 'Bart,' he said when I called, 'How long are you staying here? I would love to show you our stables. We talked a lot at the table. Maybe you would like to see what keeps us in this crazy business.'

I decided to accept his invitation.

The '*Criadores Del Campeones*' stables was an impressive operation. Klaus guided me through every aspect of the business, from the scientific feeding programs and the care of the vets on staff to the few ponies ready for shipment to Qatar. It took the best part of the morning. Then, when we sat down for lunch, Klaus confided in me, 'Bart, this is a great operation, but not a perfect one. To be perfect, we need to step it up a level. It is asking the kind of investment that the results of the present size does not produce, but it would be increasing our profits significantly.'

Where is this going, I thought, but it was not too difficult to guess.

'Are you the owner?' I asked. 'No, my father and a colleague are, I am running the show and am getting more shit than salary, but it is the kind of business that gets under your skin. There is no equal to the reputation of Argentinian polo ponies, and the global demand is only increasing.'

'Are you making a proposal, Klaus?' I asked, not wanting to beat around the bush.

'I may, Bart, if you are interested and if my father buys into my plans for the needed expansion.'

'Why are you not contacting Argentinian investors? Is it because I know next to nothing about this business?' I know it was not the nicest thing to say, but I needed honesty.

'Fair enough, Bart, I expected that question, but the answer is simple. There are many secrets in this breeding business. Inviting a partner from here is inviting trouble when you have to open the place for due diligence. As a businessman, you may understand that.'

'What about due diligence, though, Klaus? I may not know much about horses, but I understand numbers,' I said.

When I told Paisley about the conversation, her comments were rather non-committal but not negative either. 'It's up to you, sailor. I think I know the business, I know the global demand, and it is significant. *Criadores Del Campeones* has a good reputation, but yes, I can see how an expansion could increase their supply of champions. I can give you all the knowledge I have for free, sailor, but you're on your own deciding if this is for you.'

19

A bit to my surprise, the due diligence looked surprisingly good, and I could see from the numbers how an increase of scale would positively impact the results. Paisley went over the technical information and was very impressed. I was older but still young enough, and my money in the bank gave me negligible returns since the money market under the influence of Greenspan's monetary policies had lowered interests to a few percent. After the short period in my house in Holland, I knew that I was not ready yet to retire, I still needed a challenge, and the one that presented itself seemed to fit the bill.

'Would you stay with me if I accept their proposal?' I asked Paisley, knowing the answer.

'Not a chance in hell, sailor,' she answered with a smile, 'I wouldn't stand a chance against these Argentinian beauties ogling you. No Bart, I have to go home to take care of my business there and be close to my dad, who is getting older and frail. I will come and visit you from time to time if you promise you'll do the same.'

So what else is there to say? Paisley went home, and I went to the Dutch embassy to ask for their assistance in finding a reliable law firm. They gave me three addresses, and after meeting all three, I felt most comfortable with the second one, who'd never worked for *Criadores del Campeones,* or any member of the Von Schweringen family.

After having an accountant's firm recommended by *Bufete de Abogados Luzzato,* the law firm I selected, confirm Klaus's numbers, I became a forty percent owner of the company.

The book value of Criadores was fourteen million dollars, and I paid four million for my share.

I was surprised that Klaus' father and his colleague were not present during the signing of the document at Luzato's office, but Klaus carried the proper proxies, and the corporate lawyers of the company were present, so all parties signed off on the deal. I had transferred to a client's account at Luzzato the four million, and my lawyer handed over a certified bank cheque in that amount. After shaking hands, Klaus invited me for a drink later in the afternoon, which I accepted.

We toasted the transaction in *Gran Bar Danzon* later that day. 'Klaus,' I said, 'I found it a bit strange that your father and his colleague, a Mr Hochstadt, I understand from the documents, were not present during the transaction selling forty percent of their company. Why was that?'

'Yes, I understand,' Klaus answered, 'We discussed it, but my father and Hochstadt thought I deserved the honour; I found the new partner, and they did not want to take the limelight.

The new expanded and modernized company is a thing for

the next generation in their opinion, and they elected not to be present, take the role of investors and let me run the show.'

'I see. Well, I assume I will meet them soon enough. For now, I have a few priorities of my own.

In the meantime, when you have a final draft of the expansion, I would like to see it, ok?'

'Sure, Bart, I will, and if I can help you with anything here in Buenos Aires, let me know, will you?'

I found a house in Recoleta that was available for rent because the owners went overseas to work for Shell. The house was way too big but well designed and well built and came completely furnished. What was even better, there was an experienced staff of three. A woman of about fifty with a sunny demeanour was in charge, and there was a younger woman who did the laundry and cooking and boy, did she cook! Lastly, there was a man who did a bit of everything, an early retired police officer as it turned out, maintaining the house, the garden and driving my car. I also got myself a dog, a big well trained German Shepherd that for some reason quickly accepted me as his boss and soon took to sleeping beside my bed.

I liked Buenos Aires, there were great restaurants, the people were very friendly and the prices low. There were great artists also, and I bought a few paintings and carvings to give the house that was now my home a bit of a different touch. Every now and then, I visited the Criadores stables, where the expansions were underway. Klaus would walk me around the place, introduce me to staff, show me some young horses, but it was still all weird science to me. I expected that my personal involvement was not really needed at this point, so I decided to go and surprise Paisley, but the surprise was on me."

Bart kept silent.

There had been emotion in his voice when he said the surprise was on him. Harry assumed it had been an unpleasant one, so he decided to leave the old sailor with his thoughts.

"I had a surprise too," Harry said when Bart seemed to be stuck in sad memories.

"It was on a Friday in June. I remember because we, my men and I, were repairing the damage the construction workers did when they built the glasshouses over there, where the pond was.

A young boy, maybe thirteen or fourteen, just stood there staring at what we were doing. Finally, I decided to find out what his interest was all about. 'I am Jean Claude', he said in a timid voice, 'You are my Opa'. It took me completely off guard. I had a closer look at the boy's face, and now I saw an unmistakable likeness with my son when he was that age, and still a likeable child. It was the first time that I saw any of my son's children, but that was not the boy's fault, I assumed. In spite of myself, a sudden warm feeling came over me, 'So, Jean Claude,' I said, 'what a pleasure to see you. I often wondered how you would be doing. You look very much like your father when he was your age.' I indicated to my men that I would be gone for a while.

'Come, Jean Claude,' I took the young boy's hand, 'Come let

us sit over there and talk; I want to know all about you.' That *over there* was this same bench you and I are sitting on now, I sat there, where you are sitting and Jean Claude here." Harry pointed at the right side of the bench.

"But when we sat down, the boy started to cry, he cried his heart out and feeling that something was terribly wrong, I put my arm around his shoulder and held him close until he finally stopped with a few final sobs. 'What is it boy, tell me, how can I help you?' I asked.

'It is my Dad, he is very sick, and I don't know what to do. Mom left Daddy a long time ago, and we went with her. But then Mom found a new husband who wanted us to call him Dad. He was always nice to my sister and kissed her; that's when we went back to daddy. My sister Françoise and I are alone. We take care of Daddy, but now he is really sick, and I am afraid he is going to die.' He started crying again. 'Did you call a doctor?' I asked. 'Yes sir, we did, and he came several times, but he said Father needs special food. The doctor wrote it down, hypoalimentation, which means he did not eat enough.' 'Can't you feed him if he does not eat himself?' I asked stupidly, but the tears started again, 'I have not eaten myself for two days, sir, and not Françoise either,' he cried. It broke my heart. Now I realized my son and his children must have been living in abject poverty.

I felt ashamed and guilty. Here was my grandson, and he was starving. I told my men I would be gone for the day, 'Show me where you live, Jean Claude, come, let's go.' I took my handkerchief, dried his tears, took his hand, and we left the park. There is a sandwich store on the corner, so I stopped first to buy the boy a sandwich that he devoured, then ordered to wrap half a dozen of them to take with us.

My son had not been able to overcome the shame of being disbarred, nor had he been able to find an alternative source of income. Moreover, his qualifications were too tied to his previous profession, and all his former friends were gone or didn't want to know him anymore.

I found him in bed, in a small third-floor apartment in the poorest part of town, where people from The West, from Turkey and Morocco lived, in rent-subsidised dilapidated dwellings.

I was shocked to see him, much older than his years, emaciated like the pictures I had seen of concentration camp survivors. When he saw me, he cried, not able to lift his head from the pillow. I took him in my arms, and we cried together. Words were not needed; we both had been wrong, we both were sorry, we both forgave.

I was able to help, not in a big way, but I was living alone in the same house where my children were born and grew up, now my son and my grandchildren moved in with me. I nourished him slowly back to health and just loved my grandchildren. It brought new life to my home. Jaap found a job as a legal advisor with a welfare organization and regained his self-esteem.

One day he asked if he could talk to me, 'Dad, how can you ever forgive me?' he asked in a broken voice, but I had already."

Harry fixed his gaze on the spot in front of the glasshouses, where his grandson stood years ago, changing his life with four simple words, *'You are my Opa'*.

Bart awoke from his reverie.

"She was going to get married," he said resolutely as if he had just accepted the fait accompli. "To the stable boy, who was more a manager of her stable and definitely not a boy. He was actually a very nice guy, with an easy laugh and fun to drink a beer with. I should have been happy for Paisley, who was not that young anymore but still in good shape, charming and well-groomed, to say in her terms. She was hesitant to tell me. That's why she never wrote or called and was very relieved when I convincingly lied that I was happy for her. Inside I was hurt.

Should I have married her? She sure would have agreed at a certain time when our friendship became a relationship. But, would my life have been different being landlocked? Had I been too egocentric to value my freedom so much that I did not see how it impacted sweet, loyal, lovable Paisley? It was not jealousy but pain that made me decide to go back sooner than planned. I could not watch the intimacy between her and that other man, the laughter they shared, the way they looked into each other's eyes.

I said goodbye and promised to be at her wedding, but I never made it.

20

Half a year later, the extension of the stables in Buenos Aires was finished, and they had done a fantastic job.

It did not take specific knowledge to notice the difference with the old facility. Klaus was beaming when he showed me around. 'Look at the lab now, Bart. The preservation process of the semen is one of our great secrets. One day, we will make more money from that than from selling ponies. Come, let me show you something interesting.' We walked to a separate section of the stables, where foals and yearlings were kept. There were five foals in adjacent stalls, absolutely identical. 'Clones,' Klaus explained, without further comments, 'that, Bart, could make us a global leader in the breeding business.'

I felt confident that my decision to invest in the company had been a good one. Klaus seemed capable, enthusiastic and everything that we agreed should be done after my financial participation, was indeed done. Of course, I still thought about Paisley now and then, but it gradually became less and less.

During a polo game that I regularly visited, now being

recognized as an insider, I met a very charming woman. She was a rather famous painter in Argentina, whose brother played a handicap 8 in the national team. Her name was Carmen, and she was a stunning, very spirited woman. We somehow got along very well and became good friends. She increased my interest in the arts, took me to Teatro Colón where the opera Carmen played and introduced me to a group of very interesting people we often dined with in one of the excellent restaurants. She even taught me how to dance. Soon enough, I learned to speak Spanish and life in Buenos Aires actually became very pleasant.

The first full year-end showed forty percent growth in the net results and an increased demand for both ponies and semen. As a result, the value of the company had risen appreciatively already.

But I still had not been introduced to the elusive owners of the company I owned a significant interest in.

Then one day, I received a call from Mr Luzzato, the senior lawyer and proprietor of my law firm. Mr Luzzato asked if I could come to his office for a confidential meeting and stressed the need not to let anybody know about the request. Of course, it intrigued me, but I held the old gentleman in high esteem, we often met at social events, and we became sort of friends, so I concurred and went to see him.

In his private office in the statuesque neoclassical building his law firm owned on Avenida 9 de Julio, I was introduced to two gentlemen whose names I am not free to mention. They were agents of the MOSSAD, the Israeli national intelligence agency. Mr Luzzato explained the reason for the meeting; 'Bart, I have asked you to come here to meet these gentlemen, for a very personal reason. First, what I need to tell you has, up to this point, been unimportant to mention: I am a Sephardic Jew. The gentlemen I introduced you to have convinced me that there are serious reasons for me to call this unusual meeting. They have a file on you, Bart. Don't worry, nothing but good. But what is important is that they have interviewed a gentleman by the name of Mandelbaum in Jerusalem, whose house in Amsterdam you bought. He gave positive information about you as an anti-Nazi and a person well aware of the Shoah and the suffering of our people.'

I was, of course, surprised; why would the MOSSAD have a file on me? Where was this going?

'What these gentlemen will tell you in the strictest confidence may shock you, Bart, but please hear them out.' Mr Luzzato advised me.

'Sir, thank you for listening to us', the tallest of the two started, 'we are here to ask for your cooperation. We know that you invested and became a partner in the polo pony breeding company, co-owned by a certain Mr Von Schweringen and his colleague Hochstadt.

Hochstadt's name is real. His family is of German origin but has been living in Argentina since 1897. He was a sympathizer of Adolf Hitler, but so many Germans living abroad were in those days. Von Schweringen is a different story. The name is absolutely fake. We are convinced that the person calling himself by that name is Walter Braun, ex-commander of a sub-camp of Treblinka, and known by the few survivors as *The Beast*. He is personally responsible for the murder of tens of thousands of people. We have proof that Braun escaped prosecution with the help of the Vatican Trail and ended up assisted by ODESSA in Argentina.

As you may know, ODESSA stands for *Organisation der ehemaligen SS-Angehörigen,* (Organization of former SS members)'.

I almost fell off my seat, a Nazi mass murderer, one of those despicable monsters responsible for the Holocaust, and I invested in his company? They noticed my shock and embarrassment. The shorter of the two agents interjected, 'Of course, you could not have known; they have a way of becoming respected members of society with only their cronies who also escaped justice, knowing who they really are.'

Still unable to see the consequences the information would have for me personally, I asked, 'So what is it that I can do for you gentlemen?'

'We need a recent picture of Braun to scientifically compare with the one we have on file from his time at the camp. Even better would be fingerprints and a blood sample or sputum. There is a science called DNA that is able to confirm his identity conclusively. We have located a niece of Braun in Stuttgart, who is willing to cooperate. If her DNA and that of *'Von Schweringen'* match, we have proof that he is Braun, The Beast. Then we'll take it from there.'

'Bart, do not be concerned about your investment. It is only that mass murderer they are after; Hochstadt and Klaus will continue the company,' my friend the lawyer said. But that was not the first of my concerns.

'It may sound strange, gentlemen, but I have never met Von Schweringen senior yet. I have often expressed my wish to be introduced, but there was always a plausible explanation why that had not happened yet. Though now I am starting to understand why.'

'Bart, as a forty percent shareholder in the company, you are entitled to call a special board meeting. The reason you could give is that you are pleased with the present results, as I know you are, and you have an important proposal for the board, so you insist they all be present,' Luzzado suggested. 'What could that proposal be?' I wondered aloud, 'It can't be frivolous because they would see right through it,' I said.

'Agreed, but tell them you would increase your investment, without asking for additional shares, but as a low-interest loan, to even further expand the *Criadores del Campeones* stables, that is a feasible proposition and not a commitment at all. During that board meeting, it will be possible to take a close-up photo and obtain a DNA sample.'

'How would you achieve that?' I wondered.

'With your cooperation,' the tall man answered. 'We will equip you with a hidden camera, the mini-lens of which will be a small hole in the breastpin of the International Polo Federation blazer you will wear. As for the DNA, we can have a woman serving coffee and chocotorta, something no Argentinian, imposter or not, can say no to. The lady will save the cup, spoon and fork Braun used; that is enough for us.'

I thought about the proposition, and it sounded like some spy novel. *How the hell would I pull something like that off?* But I also remembered very well what Mr Mandelbaum had told me, the incomprehensible tragedy that had happened to him, his family and millions more.

'Alright,' I said, 'I'll do it. I'll call the board meeting, and I will let Mr Luzzado know about the date; it is quite normal that I visit my lawyer the day before the meeting. So that is when you can equip me with the camera, and the day afterwards, take it off me.'

'We have to be honest, sir,' the short man warned, 'this can be dangerous, the chance that he will be suspicious is not great, but the ODESSA is a very active underground organization here, one that does not tend to take prisoners. We have to tell you that, sir.'

His advice and warning, strangely enough, made it more exciting to me, 'I understand that,' I answered, 'but it is not the first danger I faced in my life, and I feel cheated, taken advantage of. So you can count on me.'

'Thanks, Bart,' Luzzado shook my hand, 'I knew we could count on you, but be careful, my friend, don't talk about it to anybody.'

'Does Klaus know?' I asked.

'We don't know, but it is possible he does not. But on the other hand, he must have seen visitors coming to his parent's home, and he may have overheard talks. So just don't tell him anything at all.'

I left his office full of mixed emotions. Had I been stupid or just naïve to associate with a war criminal? Did Klaus target me? Did he keep his father away from me, knowing of his past?

Of course, I could not and would not talk to Carmen, but I couldn't help think *what if Paisley and I were still the close friends we once were.* I wished I could talk to her.

I had decided to drive myself instead of letting my chauffeur Alejandro take me to the meeting.

Turning into Avenida Belgrano, I noticed a black Mercedes that had been parked across from the law firm's office, following me. Of course, it could be a coincidence that the car just needed to go where I went, but my suspicion was triggered. I took a right at the first corner, then made a U-turn as if I had forgotten something. The Mercedes passed, there were two men in front. I could not tell if anybody was sitting in the back; the car's windows were dark. The Mercedes continued, and I did not see it return when I drove home.

When I'd decided to stay for a certain time in Buenos Aires, I bought a BMW, not that it mattered. Still, there were quite a number of Mercedes', BMW's and Audi's around, but now I suddenly thought, *shit, I am driving a German car, did they maybe think..* but I washed the thought from my mind.

Calling for the special board meeting a few days later, Klaus contacted me, 'Bart, what's going on?' 'A normal procedure Klaus,'

I responded, 'I have seen the minutes of several board meetings that took place before my participation in the company. With all the changes I think a meeting is necessary. I have a few ideas that I think will benefit our company, but it will be increasing my exposure, so that's why, my friend.'

'But tell me at least what you intend to propose, so I can allow our board secretary to put it on the agenda and allow my father, who chairs the meetings, to prepare for it.' Klaus pleaded.

'Klaus, what I have in mind may surprise all of you. But it is a logical extension of what you initiated yourself and which you thus far have successfully implemented. Put on the agenda, *'Proposal by shareholder'* I prefer the surprise and an open discussion but no proxies this time. I have been left out of the loop long enough as a rookie in the business, but not anymore. I have called the meeting, which is within my rights, and please make sure the invitations end up in the hands of the board members.'

That afternoon, I asked Alejandro to drive me around a bit. 'Alejandro,' I said, 'you are an ex-police officer; I have a few questions, that's why we're in the car, just keep driving. A friend from the embassy warned me that there is quite a bit of crime in the city and that certain people are specifically targeted. Do you know something about that?'

'Regrettably true, sir, but which big city where the super-rich meet so often, ogled by those who hardly make a living, would not have the same problem? As a sergeant, I often had to deal with the problem, especially when violence was involved. But what is your concern, sir?'

'Are you authorized to carry a weapon, Alejandro?'

My driver smiled, 'Sir, why do you think a retired police sergeant does odd jobs around the house, waters the Cockspur Coral trees, and drives you around? I am a professional bodyguard, sir. I was for the previous owner of the house and now for you, and I carry a gun the moment I put on my pants.' I was silent for a moment. 'Well, I am surprised, pleasantly surprised, I should say. But I better adjust your salary, which I would have done already had I known.'

'Not to worry, sir, I am receiving a pension, and I knew this moment would come. Whatever concerns you, sir, my eyes are always on you, and I have your back. I am not the only retired police officer turning personal bodyguard. We form a network, helping each other when necessary. Yes, there is a professional criminal organization with deep roots in our history; I advise you to ask your lawyer about that.'

I adjusted my bodyguard's salary retroactively, which he appreciated very much. He asked for my approval to purchase some equipment to be installed in the house and on the car; I approved the six thousand dollars he needed for it.

The next day I called Luzzado. We decided to have dinner that evening outside of town in a small taverna we both liked. There were not a lot of people yet, and we took a table in the corner. I ordered a bottle of Monte Xanic Malbec. 'What's on your mind, Bart?' my friend asked, realizing that this was not just an invitation for dinner.

'After I learned that my man of all trades was really a bodyguard,' I answered, 'I asked him a few questions. One thing I wanted to know was if there was organized crime in Buenos Aires, and he advised me to ask you. Why is that?' Luzzado looked at me without saying a word as if to decide in his mind how to answer.

'Bart,' he finally started, 'there are no coincidences in life. However, what I am about to tell you may seem unbelievable but is regrettably very true.' He moved close to me to ensure he could not be overheard, but there were only a few people in the taverna, several tables away from us.

'Yes, there is organized crime, but it is not as bad as it once was. Here we are, my friend, Jews asking you to take great risks to bring a criminal to justice who mass-murdered our people. We are warning you about the dangers of ODESSA. It is almost pathetic.'

The old lawyer seemed to age before my eyes; he was clearly uncomfortable with what he was going to tell me. 'We have to go back to 1900, Bart, that is when a Jewish criminal by the name of Simon Rubinstein came to this country. He was the initiator of a gang known as the *Ashkenazum,* a splinter group of the criminal organization operating in five continents, involved in human trafficking for the sex trade, enslaving Eastern European Jewish girls. At the pinnacle of his power, he had five hundred agents working for him – an Ashkenazi Jew like myself, for heaven's sake. It is a dark page in our history and that of Judaism. The organization no longer exists thanks to a brave Jewish woman by the name of Raquel Liberman. She was able to buy her freedom and then filed a complaint in court. However, the power of the criminal organization was significant, through complicity with the police, for example, and collusion with those in high places. The organization was dissolved in 1930. There are still smaller derivative gangs, dangerous enough but nowhere near as influential as the Askenazum gang.' Luzzado picked up his glass, swirling the dark red wine holding the tumbler against the light. He hesitated for a moment, took a sip, then, sucking air through closed teeth, he swallowed.

'My God, what a story Alex. But it has nothing to do with you. There are gangsters in every single nation and among the people of every nationality and every generation. The mafia may be associated with Italy or Sicily, but they certainly don't hold a monopoly on crime.'

He smiled, probably feeling a bit better. 'I know, my friend, but although Alexander Luzzado may not sound Jewish, the name is as much Jewish as chopped liver or the Sabbath, and very Ashkenazi. There are still people gladly remembering us of that black page in Argentinian history. But here is what is so unbelievable and so mysterious almost, you agreed to be taking risks on behalf of uncountable victims, Jewish victims, like the tens of thousands of Eastern-European Jewish sex slaves a century ago. Your life may be in danger because of the ODESSA organization in Argentina. In

1900 the culprit of human trafficking in numbers unprecedented throughout history came to Argentina from Odessa, in Ukraine.'

Now it was my turn to be silent. The coincidence felt eerie.

'Well, I am surprised with the information, but as I said, it is a century ago and history. It does answer my question, though, and I will be extra careful. To be honest, that Nazi organization ODESSA scares me more than anything. People responsible for mass murder have many reasons to silence adversaries.' When I looked out of the window, a black Mercedes with tinted glass windows drove slowly by, then increased speed and disappeared in the distance.

The board meeting was held in the large meeting room of the corporate office. I arrived early, but not early enough. The day before, at my lawyer's office, I had been equipped with the spy camera. I walked through the building to the meeting room and opened the door.

Sitting ramrod in his chair at the head of the table was an old man, devoid of an expression on his face. He fixed his gaze on mine the moment I entered, staring at me through steel-rimmed glasses. My immediate impression was negative, but that was possibly because of what I was told. Here at the head of the table, chairing the board meeting of a multi-million-dollar corporation, was a Nazi mass murderer. He emanated antipathy, and he was bald-headed in a way that suggested he had been so his whole life; his features were sharp and angular. He was dressed in a grey three-piece fishbone pattern and a red/black necktie. He pointed to a chair at the far end of the table, with a gesture of his hand and a smile, baring his teeth, but that never reached his observant grey eyes. I decided not to step up to him and shake his hand in spite of his seniority; I considered his attitude rather rude. On his right-hand side sat Klaus, looking a bit awkward, on his left, whom I assumed to be his colleague Hochstadt, who decided to get out of his chair and walk up to me with an outstretched hand. 'Welcome on behalf of the board. I am Hans Hochstadt; we are extremely curious what it is you have to tell us.' There was also a male secretary taking notes, the CFO (chief financial officer), and a woman of about sixty, dressed in a dark skirt suit. Her grey hair was tied in a bun behind her head. Feeling humiliated by the surprisingly insulting treatment, I decided not to say a word. I just sat down, waited for the opening of the meeting, the reading of the minutes of the last board meeting, and then waited till it was my turn for a presentation. While Klaus talked, I thought, '*You arrogant fucking Krauts, here I am a forty percent shareholder, being treated like a schoolboy called to the principal's office for a misdemeanour*'.

'Mr Bouman,' the chairman finally addressed me, 'may we hear the reason you called this special board meeting?' his voice sounded as if he just licked his alum stone. I decided to stand up, I was a tall person already, but I wanted to tower above that miserable old fart at the head of the table.

'Mr Chairman, as you most probably already know from the name on the four million dollar cheque the company cashed, my name is Bart Bouman. Going by the fact that you occupy that chair, I assume you must be Mr Von Schweringen.' I noticed Klaus' white face. Apparently, nobody had ever talked like that to the old authoritarian villain. However, the expression on Von Schweringen's face did not change.

'I called this special meeting, as the articles of association allow me to do, because I believe I have the right to know with whom I own this successful company. As a shareholder, I have been pleased by the implementation of the plans that were presented to me to obtain my financial participation. I am also pleased with the improving results of the company and especially its potential for further growth. Nevertheless, I have no desire to be involved in the day-to-day operations. Klaus is doing a good job, I believe, but I understand numbers. I believe that there is still a discrepancy between demand and production in an expanding world of polo, hungry for Argentinian ponies, for our Argentinian ponies. Therefore, I propose expanding further to allow our company to compete head-on with the largest breeders in the country.'

I fell silent for a moment, just for effect.

'And how, Mr Bouman, do you think we should finance that? We just invested significantly in these facilities, in the buildings and infrastructure. We intend to breed and sell polo ponies, not expand the periphery of Buenos Aires.'

I decided to ignore the arrogance.

'It is why I called for this meeting,' I continued, 'I propose to make the necessary funds available.' Everybody at the table was quiet, we were halfway in the three-hour meeting, and a woman brought in coffee and slices of chocolate cake on plates. The men on the other side of the table were using the show's intermission to talk among themselves. While he listened to the voices around him, Von Schweringen kept his stare on me.

'To answer your question in more specific terms Mr Chairman,' I said when the meeting resumed, 'I am offering to double my investment.' It was a rash statement, and I didn't have a clue how I could ever have come up with that kind of money, but I was sure they did not know that. 'And let you have eighty percent of our company, Mr Bouman?' the chairman asked with venom in his voice. I stared at him for a while, then in a low and calm voice, I said, 'No sir, I am offering a low-interest loan, the terms of which I will provide in a week, purely in the interest of our company, to allow *Criadores del Champeones* to realize its potential. I have no interest in furthering my shares and do not believe that it would enhance my position nor establish esteem in your eyes, Mr Chairman.' That was a direct attack and on purpose. A colour appeared on the enigma's face, and his eyes lit up. All eyes were on the chairman.

How could he not just thank the shareholder for his generous proposition that could benefit them all? What triggered the hostility between these two men? Finally, the chairman spoke.

'Mr Bouman, you seem to have a chip on your shoulder, and I may be the cause of that.

Your offer is generous, and I advise the board to accept it in principle. I am an old man, but not so old that I could not have come out of my chair to shake your hand, which mistake I will now correct.' He stood up from his seat and walked toward me, as I walked towards him, and we shook hands. My spy camera could never have got closer than that.

With the meeting adjourned, there were no further issues. We all shook hands while Von Schweringen senior just turned his back and left the room.

I told Alejandro to take me home immediately. I intended to visit Luzzado's office tomorrow morning. Carmen would come over that evening for a white truffle risotto dinner that my chef excelled in.

She arrived at six looking incredible with her long black hair braided and a dress that did her South American figure justice. She wore a large shawl around her bare shoulders. Carmen had asked me to go with her that evening to a concert, but I had told her that it might be a hectic day, so I politely declined. She understood.

That night at nine, I noticed that my dog was very restless, so I asked Alejandro to walk him in the garden. I suddenly heard loud, aggressive barking. A moment later, Alejandro walked in, holding my dog by its collar with his left hand, hardly controlling him, and a revolver in his right pushed in the back of the shortest of the two MOSSAD agents. 'He said you know him, sir. Maybe he doesn't know what front doors are; he jumped the back fence.'

'It's ok, Alejandro, don't worry. But thanks for being alert,' and addressing the agent, 'Good to see you, my perpetually broke and drunk cousin! Please sit down, and I'll get you a beer. How much do you need this time?' The agent just shrugged his shoulders, suddenly looking like an eternally drunk and broke cousin. Alejandro continued walking the dog.

Without words, the man removed the camera and the pin and pocketed both. 'That was quick thinking, uncle,' he smiled. 'We could use you in our service, by the way, the dishes are in our kitchen.' I understood what he was saying. 'Well, cousin,' I returned his quip, 'would you like to leave through the front door this time or over the fence again?'

'I prefer the fence, but call that ravenous beast in first, and your dog too.' We both laughed.

Luzzado drafted a loan proposal at low interest repayable in four instalments at each year-end, with the shares of Von Schweringen and Hochstadt as security. But, as intended and expected, the proposal was voted down. Then a week went by, and nothing happened.

I had been in Buenos Aires for nearly two years, and I needed a holiday. I was not hearing much from Paisley of late; her last call had been some four months earlier. When I suggested the idea to Carmen, she said, 'Bart, I think you should, you've seemed a bit stressed lately. Maybe the sea is calling you, sailor? On the other hand, I could do with a vacation too. How about the two of us going?'

'Splendid idea, girl!' I said. It was exactly what I'd had in mind. 'Any particular place on your wish list?'

'Yes,' she answered immediately, 'friends of mine told me great stories about Cabo San Lucas in Mexico. It is on the southernmost tip of the Baja California peninsula and far enough away from Argentina. I would love to go there.'

Well, of course, we did go.

Landing in San José del Cabo, we decided to stay right there; we loved the small-town feel of the charming place after the busy Argentinian metropole. Following the advice of Carmen's friends, I booked a suite in a hotel called the *Viceroy*.

Immediately upon approaching the hotel, Carmen, the artist, was mesmerized by the beauty of the place. It consisted of several well designed, very large snow-white building blocks with hardly a window on the sides facing the palm-lined avenue, but opening up facing the sea side and the wide sandy beach. The units were placed in contact with the ocean so artistically among large reflecting pools that the total formed an enormous piece of art. 'Oh my God,' Carmen exclaimed breathlessly, 'look at that composition, does it not remind you of the Sydney Opera House?' I had to agree with her observation, but at that moment, I was more interested in the suite and the restaurant. I was famished.

What else is there to say about a five-star hotel in a paradisical setting? The suite was spacious, very well furnished. The amenities the *Viceroy* offered were magnificent, and Michelin cannot afford to ignore the innovative restaurant and especially the roof terrace. We met the general manager Peter Bowling who greeted us at the entrance, and with his charming wife Kathy, they were such great hosts that we felt like the whole place was built to entertain just the two of us. Peter laughed when we asked him to extend our stay for another week. We had planned to travel a bit but decided that the hotel offered everything we might be looking for. 'No problem, sir,' he said. 'That happens all the time. We're fully booked, but don't worry, I'll take care of it.' Does it surprise you that I fell in love with Carmen there and actually proposed to her while having a sumptuous dinner in the romantic *'Birdsnest'*, a vast dome woven together from twigs, covering a top restaurant in a romantic setting? Placed in the centre of the wide reflection pool, with the white towers illuminated as backdrop, it was breathtakingly beautiful. A live band played Latin music, further adding to the atmosphere. The sommelier opened a second bottle of champagne as I asked Carmen to dance with me. 'Are you seducing me, sailor?' she smiled while in my arms. But I was not the seducer; the ambience of the place was. It was the happiest time of my life."

"So did you marry, Bart? Did a woman turn you into a landlubber? You said you never had when I told you about Anna and me." Harry sounded disappointed. He rather thought of that adventurous sailor as a bit of a scoundrel with a girl in every harbour, maybe going along with Bart's stories, he kept imagining himself in his situation, satisfying his unfulfilled dreams. A married man on solid soil, well, that was precisely what he had been himself.

"No, I didn't, but that is a different story," Bart responded.

21

"We had a wonderful time in Cabo, but three weeks away from her normal duties was long enough for Carmen. She had not immediately accepted my proposal. 'I do love you, Bart, but I am a practical woman; we are living a dream here, this hotel is paradise, and I want to be sure there is no snake hidden somewhere in a mango tree. So you think about it too, then once back in the reality of Buenos Aires, you try again, sailor, and I'll give you my answer then.' She kissed me.

Back in Buenos Aires, a surprise awaited me that I should have foreseen.

'Trouble, sir,' Alejandro said when he picked us up from the airport, and we were alone in the car after taking Carmen home. 'They have been looking for you, first Klaus and later the police, they wanted to know where to reach you, but I told them I did not have a clue. Old Von Schweringen has disappeared, and they have not heard from him since. There have been blacked-out vans in front of your house and mysterious phone calls. Right now, there is a car following us, is there something I should know about, sir?'

Alejandro sounded seriously concerned.

'If you are asking me if I have anything to do with Von Schweringen's disappearance, the answer is simple, no I don't. I have no idea who could be interested in me or why the police would want to see me, but I intend to find out,' I said. 'Just take me home, and let's see what the car following us will do. Do you think you could find out from your contacts in the police force what they want?'

'Possibly, sir, I will try.'

When we arrived at my house, the blacked-out van following us just continued without slowing down.

When I was home, I immediately called Klaus to ask him about his father's disappearance.

'Bart, can I talk to you in private? I can come to your house,' he said in a somewhat conspiring voice. But something made me hesitant. 'You know, Klaus, I just came home and don't feel well, maybe something I ate on the plane. So let me give you a call tomorrow, ok?' He reluctantly agreed.

The next morning Alejandro had some news. 'Sir,' he said while we were alone, 'I talked to a friend of mine in the force. There is a senior lieutenant by the name of Garcia who's been put on the case. The disappearance of Von Schweringen is a mystery but as yet not a criminal case. Garcia has been compromised in the past in a few cases involving ex-Nazis. Somehow, he seems to be protected from high above, over the head of the chief of police, who is a man with integrity. There were always rumours that Von Schweringen was a Nazi fugitive living under a fake identity. His lawyers claimed they were just rumours, and there was no proof of the contrary.

Not that his would have been a unique case, during Perón, a lot of these criminals bought their way into our country. It gave Argentina a bad rap, but there are many good Jewish families here, and many Argentinians hated the Nazis as much as I do. There has also been talk that Garcia is on somebody's payroll. His salary cannot explain his lifestyle, but again, nobody seems to be able to touch him. He buried himself in the Von Schweringen case as a bloodhound smelling a trail. So, please, sir, be careful. If that damned Nazi organization is involved, your life is in danger.'

'Thank you, Alejandro,' I said. 'But I am sure you'll keep your eyes on me. This information is important. I will talk to Klaus this afternoon, then wait and see if the police contact me. If they do, I will go there with my lawyer.'

'Sir, if it is alright with you, I would prefer to stay here in one of the guest rooms, and I would like to go with you wherever you go, at least until we know what the hell is going on,' Alejandro suggested. I agreed.

That afternoon Klaus came to the house; he seemed a bit nervous but not distressed. My dog didn't seem to like him. He growled and was restless, moving a bit closer to me, keeping his ears pointed and his eyes on Klaus. 'Sir, can you have a look at this?' Alejandro asked before I started listening to my visitor. So I followed him to the kitchen, 'A blacked-out Mercedes was following your visitor and slowed down in front of the house, sir,' he warned, for which I thanked him.

'Bart,' started Klaus when I sat down, 'something very secret and very sinister is going on. I don't have a clue what happened to my father, where he went or why he disappeared. It happened while you left for your holiday. I am his only son, and Mother passed away eleven years ago. So after several days of not hearing from him, I went to the house to try and see if I could find a clue, but somebody had been before me.'

'What do you mean?' I asked.

'Somebody had been in the house and had gone through my father's papers. I know because files I knew to be there had disappeared. The drawers of his desk had been forced open, and I could tell somebody had opened the safe that was hidden behind a Bavarian landscape on the wall.' He sounded sincere.

'What do you think they were after Klaus, money? Have you talked to the police?'

'Why would they take files if they were after money? No, some secret must have been hidden there. Do you have any idea, Bart?' The question surprised me. He knew very well that I hardly met his father, only that one time and I barely talked to him.

'I don't have a clue, Klaus. I didn't know your father; it's not a secret that no sympathy was lost between us. Secrets with men usually have something to do with women or money. Could it be that?'

'My father? Hell no, Bart. The closest friends he ever had were two German Shepherds like that monster at your feet keeping his eye on my jugular. No, it must be something else. Well, I guess I better go back to my office. If you happen to hear something, let me know, Bart.' I said I would and showed him out.

About an hour after Klaus left, I received a call from Lieutenant Garcia, asking me to come to the police station to answer a few questions. So I called my lawyer friend Luzzado, 'Bart,' he said, 'be careful, that Garcia is bad news. I would love to go with you, but I have a better idea. A young Argentinian associate of mine is a brilliant lawyer and ten times as smart as that crook; he'll go with you. Any particular time Garcia asked you to come?'

'Tomorrow at 2 p.m. I answered.'

Even without the briefing on Garcia, I would have disliked him the moment we entered his office. He pointed at the chair across from his table without saying a word, but we were two, so I did not sit down. 'Are you Bart Bouman?' he asked without introducing himself, 'Who's that?' he said, pointing at Julio, my lawyer. 'That Lieutenant, Garcia, if that is indeed your nameplate on the desk, is my lawyer Julio Rodriques.'

'Smart ass, eh?' he remarked while colouring a bit red in his face.

But he stood up from his throne and moved a second chair in front of his desk; we both sat down. 'We'll deal with the papers later, but tell me, what made you come to Argentina?'

Before I could say a word, my lawyer jumped in; 'Lieutenant, is my client a person of interest in a criminal case?' Garcia looked at him with scorn in his eyes. 'I am just asking Bouman a question, is there a problem with that?'

'Actually, yes, sir, there is.' Rodriques said. 'My client is a foreign national and an investor in this country. He can speak and understand basic Spanish. However, I insist that a court-approved Spanish-to-Dutch translator be made available for interrogations, which is within my client's rights. You can contact my office to let me know when a translator is available. Is there anything else, Lieutenant?' The police officer looked as if he swallowed a porcupine, made a gesture with his hand that we could leave, which is what we did, realizing that we did not exactly make a friend. 'Why was that?' I wanted to know. 'That man is a rat, Mr Bouman. He'll try every trick in the book; he could use wordplay that you would not readily pick up on. You'll have a great advantage in understanding his Spanish questions and time to think as his words are being translated. But it will take him some time to find what I insisted on.'

I had mixed feelings about the meeting. I understood that Rodriques' move had been smart, yet on the other hand, I wanted it to be over and done with. I needed to talk to somebody, so I called Carmen to meet her for dinner at El Obrero downtown. We talked about our holiday first, but she had heard about Von Schweringen's disappearance and understood that I did not come for small talk. I filled her in as much as possible without giving away anything. A few tables away from us, Alejandro kept his eyes on me. It was rather busy in the popular restaurant that evening, but before we entered, he went in first, and not noticing anything suspicious, he walked us to our table. When I went to the washroom, there were several men with similar intentions at the same time. For an instant, one of the heavy square columns in the building blocked the view to where Alejandro was. In a flash, a needle was inserted in my arm, and I was rushed out the backdoor between two men, a third covering their back. The last thing I remembered was a black van; then I passed out.

When I regained consciousness, I was sitting on a chair with my hands cuffed behind at the back, a sharp light shining in my face, and I had a splitting headache. I could not see anything beyond the glare when a toneless voice sounded from behind it, 'Mr Bouman, if that is indeed your name, it may interest you to know that we also have your girlfriend in custody at a different location in our building. But you will be able to hear her through the speaker system soon enough. Regrettably, we had to eliminate your bodyguard, though there is a chance that your fiancée will fare much better. Do you understand me? Just answer yes or no.' I elected not to say a thing.

Suddenly a scream sounded through the room, obviously from a woman in pain. It gave me a stab through my heart. 'You goddamn bastards!' I shouted, 'you hurt Carmen, and I'll find you and wring your fucking neck.' 'Of course, Mr Bouman, we understand, but let me explain. Every time you refuse to answer or are lying, I will push this button I have here, and a current will travel through the electric wires attached to your lover's genitalia

223

and nipples. From many similar cases in the past, I remember that sixteen shocks are the maximum a human body can take. Shall we try again?' 'Du verfluchter Schweinhund!' I shouted, *you cursed dog*, 'This is not your Nazi empire! You hurt my woman, and I'll blow up your whole goddamn place.' The scream that followed chilled me to the bone and brought me to my senses. I still had a throbbing headache, but I understood that I did not call the shots.

'Okay, what do you want to know?' I asked.

'That's much better,' the voice said. 'is your real name Bart Bouman?'

'Yes,' I answered.

'Why did you come to Argentina two years ago?' *So they know*, I thought.

'Because a friend introduced me to polo, and I ended up investing in a polo pony breeding company.'

'Are you a wealthy man, Mr Bouman?'

'It depends on by what standards. If your question is did I invest my own money, the answer is yes.'

'Where is Herr Von Schweringen?'

The sudden change in interrogation took me by surprise, so I hesitated a moment.

'I don't have a clue,' I answered. The scream that followed brought tears to my eyes; I physically felt a stabbing pain in my crotch. 'Stop it,' I shouted, 'It is true, I don't know. I heard of his disappearance when I returned from a holiday; why would I know anything about it?'

'What did you discuss with that Jew Luzzado?'

'With my lawyer? Business, of course. I am an entrepreneur, not a lawyer. I often need his advice; the red tape in this country is complicated enough.'

The voice was silent, I cringed, preparing myself for the fourth scream, but it didn't come.

'Before you went to Cabo San Lucas, you offered a large low-rent loan to Von Schweringen, with his shares as security. Unfortunately, we happen to know that your balance in the bank does not allow such generosity. Who was going to finance you, the MOSSAD?'

'Hell no, there are banks for that, you know, why would the MOSSAD finance me?'

'Maybe because of your contacts with them through that Jew, who only gives you business advice?' the voice suggested cynically.

'That's preposterous!' I objected.

'Where is Herr Von Schweringen?'

'Again, I don't know. I have no idea why he disappeared.'

This time the scream lasted twice as long and ended in heavy sobs.

I could not take it anymore. I could spy and help people out, but I was not heroic enough to be instrumental in the slow and beastly torture of the woman I loved. I mentally broke down.

'Ok, stop it!' I almost cried, 'Ask me what it is you want to know, I honestly don't know where Von Schweringen presently is, but other than that, just ask.' I was not very proud of myself.

'That's much better. Our methods never fail, Bouman. So tell us, what was it that the Jew needed to discuss with you in secret?'

I thought for a moment, 'He asked me if I was willing to....' but I never got to finish my sentence.

Suddenly a muffled explosion sounded from behind the light. Several shots and screams rang out, this time only from men, then silence and thankfully, the light was switched off. I heard voices but was still blinded from the wretched light and a human wreck from the interrogation and the suffering I caused Carmen. Someone untied my arms, and slowly I started to see faces. I recognized Alejandro with a gun in his hand, a man I didn't know, and then there was Carmen, who was perfectly fine. She embraced and kissed me, 'Darling, it's ok, it's over, Bart. Those monsters are dead.' I sobbed in her arms like a baby, crying, 'I'm sorry baby, I'm sorry!' But it turned out that there was nothing to be sorry about. Those damned Nazis had faked the electrocutions. They'd just got a woman to act the screams, probably laughing when she did. Needless to say, it took quite a while before I was myself again."

Harry had been listening breathlessly as if the terrible pain had been inflicted on his own body. Then again, he was also the man tied to his chair, being interrogated by a sinister voice from the past.

"What happened?" he asked needlessly, knowing instinctively that Bart would not skip a grand finale.

Bart did not immediately satisfy his curiosity. Instead, he seemed to suck the answer from his empty pipe again.

"Alejandro told me," he finally said, "immediately after I disappeared, he called a friend he knew from the police. The location where these Nazis often conferred was well known but under some mystic protection from high up. They took a considerable risk to enter the building and kill several of those Nazis. Still, paradoxically the same powers that provided the protection could do nothing about the killings because it would open up a can of worms. There was one significant change: the Federal Police removed Garcia. There were several house-calls on suspected ODESSA members, but they never killed the snake's head. The organization is too extensively interwoven among the fabric of the Argentinian nation.

Braun was taken to Israel by the MOSSAD, prosecuted, proven guilty and executed, but without much publicity. As it turned out, Klaus was well aware of his father's Nazi past. He was even involved in certain activities with the ODESSA. As a result, Hochstadt withdrew his investment in the company, and within a year, the company was bankrupt."

"So you lost all your money again?" Harry asked unbelievingly.

"Yep," Bart answered as if it was just an unimportant detail.

"What about Carmen? Did you marry her?"

"No, I didn't. I realized that my life was still in danger in Buenos Aires, so I went to Holland and moved back into my house on the Heerengracht. I tried to call her, sent a few letters, but never heard from her again."

"So what did you do then?" asked Harry, hardly believing that this was the end of the adventures.

"Not what I *did,* Harry, but what I am doing," Bart answered, preparing himself for his final narrative, "It's what I am doing now, man, and maybe you can be part of it."

22

Harry could not believe his ears.

"Me?" he exclaimed, pointing at himself, "I am not a businessman, Bart. I don't have any money, and I am too old to travel. So what do you mean by maybe I can be part of it? I am just an ordinary gardener."

"That's exactly why, man," Bart waved away the objections of the man next to him. "No money needed from you and no travelling either. My next project is right here, where you and I are sitting." Bart sounded even more enthusiastic than he did the entire day.

"Here? You mean here in Amsterdam?"

"Not just Amsterdam, I mean here, in the Vondelpark."

Harry was dumbfounded. There was undoubtedly no gold under the rich soil here, not enough trees to start a lumber business either. Even if the pond had still been there, it might have contained sticklebacks, but definitely no shrimps. So what the hell was that old sailor talking about?

"What business could you do here in the park, Bart?" he asked.

"Not in the park, but with the park," Bart explained. "The

city has grown and continues growing. There are millions and millions of tourists coming every year visiting what is known as The Venice of the North. This park is smack in the centre of the canals encircling the old city, and you know what it is used for?"

Harry did not consider it a real question, so he did not answer.

"I'll tell you what it's used for," Bart continued, "It's a place for old farts like you and me to sit on a bench and talk, wasting our time. It's a place for mothers to get out of the house to talk to other mothers sitting on the grass while kids are romping around them. It's a place where at night, philanderers can be found screwing behind your lilac bushes. That's all it is, Harry. Now listen to what it is going to be. I have all the plans ready on paper.

There is a dramatic parking problem in the city. There is only a limited number of parking spots along the canals, but people keep coming to the metropole like pigeons to the park. You can tell them not to, or to come by train or bus, but the majority won't listen. So what I am proposing is to build an enormous parking area covering the entire park, except for that cluster of old trees in the centre, that part remains open. It won't be just a massive concrete block, no sir, it will follow the rounded lines of the park. The entire construction will be on columns taller than those trees there, and the six parking levels will be accessible from two sides through ramps. But the first floor will be only for shops, the second floor for restaurants, entertainment and nightclubs, and the rooftop will be an enormous green area with terraces. It will be planted with trees and large flower pots, many shaded areas to sit and paths to stroll, fountains and ponds and at night it will be bathing in light and live music will be playing all over the place". Bart started to use wide gestures with both arms as if he were creating his vision from the air, right there while sitting on the old park bench.

"No!" Harry exclaimed, "You can't do that, man, that's nonsense. The park is not at all what you say it is. Many people, old and young, use it; it belongs to the people of Amsterdam, you take away their park, and there'll be a mutiny. How could you do that? My whole life, I cared for this place; I planted and cared for everything you see around us. This is an oasis in this busy town, and you can't destroy that man." Harry was livid. What was this sailor talking about? "Besides, you would never have the money for a stupid idea like that!" he added.

"Ah, my friend, and here you are wrong. I never put all my money in that polo adventure. There was enough left to pay an architect for the presentation plans, which is what I did. I have had three meetings already with the city planning committee and the counsellor of public works. I also talked to investment bankers who are very interested in this multi-billion-dollar project and are convinced that a public offering of shares will be well received by the market."

"On Sundays, it is always jam-packed," Harry said softly as if Bart never talked, "Families come with their children to picnic on the field. That day you don't smell the flowers but the delicious fumes of barbequed chicken or hamburgers. If you happen to stroll by, they offer you a bun with something and sometimes, they just ask you to sit down and join them. Some play music, and you hear laughter all over the park."

"You may wonder how we can make money on a project like that," continued Bart, "let me tell you. We'll appoint different real estate companies because it will be too big for one company alone. The commercial floor will be completely sold, preferably to one investor, but if the market prefers to buy the individual units, that's fine too. We'll make a nice bit of money on that and repay a good part to the bank who financed the project." Harry didn't seem to have heard him at all.

"Sometimes young couples get married in the park, especially in spring when the Syringa Vulgaris are in bloom, the lilacs. They're permitted to put up a wedding tent, and all the guests take pictures of the bride and groom in front of the flowers. It always puts a smile on the face of passersby." Harry directed his gaze to the Lilac bushes, where he had seen so many happy young people tying the knot. "Chuppahs too", he added, not to forget the Jewish weddings.

"Not the parking area," warned Bart. "That's where the real money is. The parking area we'll keep, and there won't be any free parking, no sir." He seemed to have missed entirely the fact that his neighbour on the bench had been talking too. "The parking alone will take in so much cash that within five years, the bank is paid back in full, with interest. From then on, it is a cash cow shitting money. We'll be like Rockefeller, man."

But Harry ignored his optimism.

"The Monday's were always school days for the little ones," he said, looking out of dreaming eyes. "The kindergarten, the lowest classes of the primary schools and also the kids from the children's hospital in West. Seeing those puppies play made my Monday easy. Anna was still alive then, 'Har' she said, she always called me Har, 'you have to ask your boss if you can build a small petting zoo, with lambs, goats, Bambi's, those mini horses, and a calf!' So I did, and for many years the little ones loved it. But then some old bitch in the city decided it was animal cruelty, and we had to take it down. I still can hear the kids cry about it. What about toddler cruelty, I thought." Harry let out a deep sigh.

"I didn't even talk about the roof park yet," said Bart undisturbed. "I call it roof park because it will be all green, what you see, and you'll plant it, Harry. Trees in containers, flowerbeds, grass areas and tulip beds. We won't sell that part either, but just rent out parts of it, the golf driving range, for example, and the canoe pond. The nightclubs will be permanent because a city needs nightlife, I have it all on paper, man, and we'll start as soon as the licences are issued, two months max, they told me. So we can start before summer."

Bart straightened his cap, put his pipe back between his teeth to indicate this story was finished. He made a final gesture with his hand by way of an exclamation point behind a sentence.

Harry kept silent. He bent forward on his side of the bench, both hands folded like in prayer, clamped between his knees, a worried expression on his face. Then he straightened up. He let his gaze wander over the Syringa Vulgaris, the Gladiolus Palustris, the Rhododendron Ferrugineum, all those trees, shrubs and plants he knew by name. He had cared for them his whole life like a shepherd cared for his flock. It would all be replaced by concrete. He felt a heavy weight on his heart.

Bart was done. There were no further details he could think of, and with a satisfied smile, he leaned back and smoked his empty pipe. Then a thought seemed to hit him. Turning to the man sitting on the bench next to him, he said;

"Billy was a bit of a daredevil, it cost him his life." He seemed to chew on those last words as if he pictured the tragic death of Billy still happening right in front of him.

The sun had long disappeared behind the trees lining the boundaries of the park. The birds could be heard warbling, twittering or chirping the day goodnight. Some late joggers ran along the empty paths undisturbed by cyclists or strollers.

Two nurses approached the old men, still sitting on the bench, "Come, grandpa," the first one addressed Bart in a somewhat derogatory and authoritative voice. "Time for your medicine. You have been out long enough today." Then to Harry, "Did he bother you, sir?" Harry could just slowly shake his head. Then, willingly like a young child, Bart walked away from the bench, holding on to the nurse's arm for support.

Harry kept staring at the disappearing adventurer, "What an

incredible life", he remarked when the second nurse was just about to follow her colleague. It stopped her in her tracks.

"Who, Bouman? Bart Bouman?" she seemed surprised.

"Yes, that old sailor, what a fascinating life he lived, travelling to all corners of the globe and sailing the oceans of the world, what a globetrotter."

The nurse roared with laughter, "That globetrotter is the retired lighthouse keeper of Terschelling Island, like his father before him. He had never been off that island his whole life until he came to our care facility. In his solitude, he has read a lot, history books, journals, travelogues, and he likes to make people believe he experienced it all himself."

The woman walked away, shaking her head, still slightly amused.

Harry stood up from the bench, ready to shuffle home, still confused but feeling much better now, carrying a smile on his wrinkled old face. At least his Vondelpark would not be covered in concrete, and his beloved Syringa Vulgaris would survive.

* * * * * * *